Donald McFarlan was born in Glasgow in 1952. A 'son of the manse', he was educated at Glasgow Academy and Cambridge University where he read English. In a varied career in publishing he has been, *inter alia*, Editor of the Penguin Classics and of *The Guinness Book of Records*. He is also the author of *The Guinness Book of 'Why?'*, a book about the science of everyday things.

Rob Roy

A novelization by
Donald McFarlan

Based on the motion picture written by
Alan Sharp

HEADLINE

First published in 1995
by HEADLINE BOOK PUBLISHING

10 9 8 7 6 5 4

ISBN 0 7472 5106 1

Typeset by Keyboard Services, Luton, Beds

Printed and bound in Great Britain by
Cox & Wyman Ltd, Reading, Berks

HEADLINE BOOK PUBLISHING
A division of Hodder Headline PLC
338 Euston Road
London NW1 3BH

Rob Roy

Contents

PROLOGUE

The snake which swallowed a porcupine

The year is 1714. It is obvious to all concerned that Queen Anne has reached the last few months of her life and, there being no obvious heir on the horizon, the Court at London is awash with rumour and speculation.

While these great affairs of State might seem remote from the banks of Loch Lomond or the Braes of Balquhidder, here too they are to have an impact. Scotland is adjusting to the effects of a disastrous Act of Union with her southern neighbour. This treaty, negotiated for commercial gain by a self-serving new mercantile class which wishes to further its expansionist ambitions by facing southwards, has sounded the death knell for the traditional way of life of the Highlander. This is a fate from which it is never to recover, as is to be underlined by the final, ignominious Jacobite defeat in 1746, when the reality of economic colonialism finally comes to the fore.

As is usual in any border territory, these stresses are nowhere more to be felt than along that part-cultural, part-geological divide known as the Highland Line, where the wild Highlander – his own economy in jeopardy – finds it all too tempting to make a brief excursion to rieve a few cattle from his newly-prosperous Lowland neighbour.

Against this backcloth, then, an unlikely cattle drover was to become caught up in the personal feud between two powerful protagonists; John Campbell, second Duke of Argyll, and James Graham, first Duke of Montrose, whose families' enmity had already flared up over several generations.

That cattle drover is our hero – Robert Roy of the clan Gregor.

Chapter One

On the Braes of Balquhidder

And thus among these rocks he lived,
Through summer's heat and winter's snow:
The eagle, he was lord above,
And Rob was lord below.

It was early evening and, although the peaks were still bright, in the valleys the light was slowly transmuting by a gradual process of reverse alchemy from golden clarity to the melancholy leaden grey so typical of a Highland gloaming. A band of half a dozen or so men was making its way down the steep sides of a glen and across the stream at its foot. Although they were travelling fast and at a steady lope, they looked tired and seemed to bear many of the stains of hard travel. They were dressed in a plaid of varying shades of dun and dusky green – colours which toned naturally with the heathers and brackens of the hillside, and with the lichens of the rocks and the trees. To a man, all were armed with broadswords, daggers and pistols. One or two had small deerskin targes slung behind.

One man was slightly older and taller, and from his bearing he was obviously their leader. He was bearded and long-haired and had a quick, intelligent face. Rob Roy, for it was he, stopped and picked something up from the ground and sniffed at it. It was a piece of cattle dung which he then passed to another of the men.

He looked attentively at the other man and asked, 'McDonald, how long . . . ?'

McDonald took the piece of dung, and with all the loving care of a connoisseur broke open its friable surface, crumbled it between forefinger and thumb, sniffed at the still moist interior, put a piece in his mouth, spat it out, and then pronounced, 'A day . . . maybe two, Rob.'

Another of the band, a much younger man, Alasdair, who had been watching this procedure with some impatience, burst out, 'Ach! They're away and gone, Rob, and the beasts sold.'

Rob, who had been scanning the skyline at the far side of the glen, appeared not to hear this, but continued to survey the now darkening ridge. The others crowded round, awaiting his word. Eventually he slowly turned in order to address them thoughtfully.

'There's a wee glen over on the other side of Ben Dubh. If I was a tink with a two days' start, I'd lie up there and kill me some meat.'

The others were taciturn as they absorbed this but eventually one of them said, 'We'd not get there before dark, Rob.'

'Not stood here we won't, Gregor!' and Rob moved on almost before he had finished speaking. The men looked at each other, and without demur followed him at a fast lope up the punishingly steep far side of the glen. It was fast growing dark, and by the time they were looking down on their destination the night was almost pitch black.

It was a small steep-sided gully, which made a natural corral for the two or three dozen small and wiry cattle that were penned in behind a rope. A little further off was the carcass of a cow, which had already been partially butchered. In front of this a fire was burning, and around it squatted a ring of nine or ten men. All of them were holding pieces of meat, skewered on sticks and dagger-points, in the flames of the fire. They were a feral-looking crew, much more ragged than their pursuers, with faces marked by desperation and hunger. Among them sat a woman, as voracious as any of the men and similarly clad.

One man stood outside the circle and watched out into the darkness. This vigilance and his solitude marked him out as some kind of leader. After a moment he turned towards the circle. He stared at the snarling, chewing pack and, reaching in, took a piece of meat from one of them and put it in his own mouth. The deprived man protested loudly, but the leader merely met this protest with a mock baleful look, and then cut the meat off close to his mouth with a practised slice. The man who had lost his supper got up with a curse and repaired to the larder to cut himself another steak.

Rob and McDonald were looking down into this little arena where the fire made a lurid tableau.

'Rob, you can smell them through the meat.'

Rob considered this. 'Aye, if they fought as strong as they smelled, we'd be in trouble.'

Alasdair came crawling up to join them, and in a mixture of youthful wonder and sycophancy, exclaimed, 'Just like you said, Rob . . . there they are!'

Rob let this go, but McDonald could not resist a sardonic observation and said quietly, 'I thought they were away and gone and the beasts sold, Alasdair Roy.'

Alasdair was hurt at this and looked at Rob to see how his leader had reacted, but Rob had other thoughts on his mind. He had seen all he needed, and silently crawled back down the slope, followed by McDonald. Smarting from the rebuke, the younger Alasdair let the other two go on their way and lay for a moment longer staring at the scene below . . .

The rustlers had sated their hunger – or at least in one respect. A squabble was breaking out over the woman, who sat gnawing at a rag of meat. The leader cursed the two disputing men to be silent and beckoned the woman towards him. She went over, as obedient as a dog, and lay down by him as the other men settled down into their plaids. Alasdair caught a glimpse of her face – a slack, half-witted look – and he continued to watch from the hillside, suddenly interested in the doings below.

Meanwhile, a couple of hundred yards away over the ridge, Rob and the others were sitting in a tight circle. Their plaids were pulled up around their shoulders and their feet held to the tiniest of fires, as they passed round a ram's horn of aquavit and ate oatmeal from their cupped hands.

Two schools of thought seemed to be developing among the younger men. The more confident was that of Coll: 'We can rush them when they're asleep.'

Meanwhile Iain expressed his doubts. 'Ten of them to six of us . . . ?'

McDonald pointed out, 'Nine. One of them's a woman.'

Gregor was of the full-blooded persuasion: 'Half of them would be dead before they were awake.'

At this point Alasdair returned, excited by the news he bore. 'They're taking turns shagging that whore they have with them.' He held out his hands to the fire, more for dramatic effect than for warmth, and then, turning to Rob, continued obsequiously: 'How are we going to take them, Rob?'

Rob didn't say anything for a moment, and then, wearily, 'I'll go and talk to them in the morning.'

The others were baffled and Coll, perhaps embold-ened by the aquavit, voiced their confusion after a momentary silence. 'What's to say to a bunch of thieving tinks, caught with the beasts?' And he shrugged.

Rob got to his feet. 'I'll think on something.' And he went, heart-weary at the conversation, to find himself a place to lie down. The others, with the exception of Alasdair, did the same. He sat where he was for a while, then, when the others had gone, lay down as close to the warmth of the fire as he could get and silently pondered the events of the night.

McDonald had lain down behind Rob and was wrapping himself in his plaid. After a moment's silence Rob said, 'I'm getting too old for this, wet-arsed in the heather chasing other men's cattle.'

'Then come away to the Americas with me.'

It was a sore point, and Rob had heard McDonald in this vein before, but he said nothing to this as McDonald went on: 'They say there's fine acres for the clearing in Virginia.'

'Aye, and they'll likely be as hard as these to sleep on,' and he closed his eyes, his tone not encouraging further comment.

McDonald lay for a moment and then, unwilling to let the conversation end on this tone, asked, 'Why are you going in to talk to them?'

'I know one of them,' Rob replied flatly.

It was early, and in the thin dawn light of the morning the cattle thieves were still asleep around the fire, which had burned down to a grey circle of ash. The cattle were down on their knees behind the rope, blowing soft rags of steam from their nostrils. Something brought one, then another, then the rest, to their feet, staring into the chill morning mist.

It was Rob, striding into the camp and making no

effort at concealment. In spite of the cold he was not wearing his plaid, and his left hand was hooked in the basket handle of his claymore, which jutted out behind him like a tail. He went within ten paces of the circle and called out, in a loud, clear voice, 'Up, up you bunch of ragged-arse tinker cow thieves, this is Robert Roy McGregor.'

The leader, who had been sleeping a little apart from the rest of the pack, was the first to start up as Rob went on, '. . . Come to reclaim the thirty-two beasts stolen from His Lordship, James Graham, Marquis of Montrose.'

And the leader was fully on his feet now, sword in hand, and staring around into the mist. There was no sign of any of the rest of Rob's men. The other tinkers were unwillingly rousing themselves now with widely varying degrees of alacrity. The woman untangled herself from the plaid of the last man who had used her, and stared out in a somewhat bovine way. Rob paid them no attention but looked straight at the man before him, who, it was clear, recognized him. Rob addressed the tinker. 'So it's you, Sibbald, still at your mooching . . . ?'

Rob looked at the others, who were blearily looking around to see how many men Rob had with him. 'Throw down now and I'll spare you . . . all but one,' and he fixed his gaze ironically back on Sibbald. 'Not terms likely to appeal to you, Tam, but there's a price to being a leader of men.'

His mockery had been light, almost commiserating,

but it goaded Sibbald into moving into an attacking stance – his sword held low and extended.

'By God, McGregor, if there's killing to be done, you'll be the first.'

Rob stood erect and unruffled, his left hand hooked casually in the guard of his claymore, his right down by his side, fingers loose. He watched Sibbald steadily as he began to inch forward, coming into range.

The rest of the gang were now fully up on their feet, and were glancing around nervously into the surrounding darkness. Only the woman remained on the ground, slackly curious.

Sibbald closed on Rob. 'Just who is it you think you are, acting the great chief – and you as big a thief as any of us?'

'And a better one than you'll ever be. If I had stolen His Lordship's cattle, you would not have come walking into my dreams so easy.'

The others were now alert, weapons in hand, and awaiting the outcome of this encounter. Sibbald made a menacing sweep of his blade, cocking it. Rob didn't move but stood motionless. His voice dropped until he was conversing only with the man in front of him.

'I can call the Gregorach, Tam, and kill the half of you, or it can be between us and nothing more.'

Sibbald stared back at him, fear beginning to seep through his defiance. Rob seemed to lean closer as he almost whispered, 'Think on it, man. Are you not better dead this morning after a good hump and a belly full of stolen beef . . . or would you have me march you back to

Montrose so you can shit yourself on the gallows a month hence?'

The calm, almost sympathetic voice snapped Sibbald's control and he came at Rob with a lunging, overhead slash. Rob seemed barely to move, only bending enough for his fingers to pluck the short *skian dhu* from the top of his hose. He then stepped deftly inside and beneath the swing of Sibbald's sword and stabbed upwards below Sibbald's ribs with a terrible, controlled thrust.

His left arm went round Sibbald's neck, holding him on to the blade which he worked savagely, twisting it in the man's body. Blood gushed from Sibbald's mouth, choking any words. Rob held him almost in an embrace . . . until the other man went limp. Then he looked beyond the dead man to where the rest of the tinkers stood as if transfixed.

'Throw down now, and you have my word that no more will die.'

They stared at each other, leaderless and trying to find common cause. Rob called out the order to the Gregorach into the mist beyond the tinkers, 'Come, lads . . . and if there's any man with a blade in his hands – then cut him down.'

At this, the first swords dropped. The Gregorach came looming out of the mist from a wide arc around the gully.

At last Rob released his hold of Sibbald, and the body fell away from the knife. At this point the rest of the gang quickly threw down, totally bereft of any resistance.

Suddenly a new sound tore into the bleak morning air

as the woman screamed. She was staring at the rest of the tinkers like a mad thing, and yelling her hatred and contempt of them. 'Are ye men, or what are ye? He kilt Tam and you stand by and let him . . . and him as much an outlaw as any of you!'

She seized up a short sword and ran at Rob, who caught her arm and turned her round, pinning her. He had to avert his head at the rank stench of her breath as she struggled and kicked and screamed at the shuffling men. 'Not a man among you . . . your mothers curse you, you spittle, you leavings—'

Rob clamped a hand over her mouth and silenced her.

There was no further resistance from the terrified rabble, and it was a matter of little consequence for the Gregorach to tie them together with a rope behind their backs – with the dead man tied to them. The woman was gagged and tied up separately while the cattle were rounded up and readied for driving back over the ridge.

Rob walked around the prisoners, talking in a low but urgent voice. 'Listen to me well and remember this, for I will remember you, every last one . . . when next you think to steal cattle, have a care they are not under my protection. For if they are, you are not stealing from their owners, you are stealing from me, Robert Roy McGregor, and no man steals my beasts and makes a profit. If you doubt me, ask Tam Sibbald.'

He took a knife from his waist band and commanded, 'Up on your feet!'

They struggled to rise as Rob turned and threw the knife as far down the slope as he could. It briefly flashed in the morning light before disappearing into the heather. They stared blankly after it, then back at Rob who walked away and headed over to the woman.

The circle of men started down the hill after the knife, every one of them trying to face the front, dragging the corpse of Sibbald among them. It was inevitably a scene without much dignity in it.

Alasdair stood near the woman, his face wrinkled up in disgust. He looked at Rob as he came up. 'What are you going to do with her?'

Rob leant down, cut the rope which bound her wrists and quickly stepped back. The woman scrambled up and backed away from both of them.

'Be on your way, and tell no man you fared ill at our hands.'

She stared at Rob for a moment, then turned tail and ran after the others.

Alasdair grimaced. 'What a hudder! Did you smell her?'

McDonald came back down as the last of the cattle went safely over the hill. He looked down the slope at the struggling heap of men and commented wryly, 'Scotland to the very mark, eh . . . ?'

Rob smiled at the conceit, but apprehensive that this line of thought might be turning towards the all too well-charted waters of further speculation on the benefits of the Americas, turned away without any comment. Relieved at the outcome of the morning's work, they talked easily as they sauntered back down the hill to take up with the cattle again.

Alasdair turned round and watched as the woman caught up with the struggling circle of men. She then ran past them to where she thought the knife had fallen, and started to search as the men came stumbling and cursing towards her. Then with a cry of delight she found the knife and held it up. Alasdair was alarmed and he turned to tell Rob, but his leader had gone.

Behind him, Alasdair could hear the men below shouting to the woman to bring them the knife. He looked back again as the woman held it up, taunting them and shrieking at them. As they tried to rush towards her, with a yell of defiance and glee she hurled the knife even further down the hill and ran in order to get away from their wrath.

Alasdair stared and shook his head. 'What a hudder . . .' And he ran to catch up with the rest of the party, agog with the burden of the tale he had to tell.

CHAPTER TWO

The champions

Heaven gave Rob Roy a dauntless heart
And a wondrous length and strength of arm:
Nor craved he more to quell his foes,
Or keep his friends from harm.

Inside the cavernous and somewhat shabby hall of a large country house a noisy crowd was milling about. It was a curiously mixed bag of very different types indeed. Among the more identifiable figures of aristocrats, hawkers and vendors, mingled an assortment of clansmen of widely varying demeanour and degree. The atmosphere was a social one, but there was a *frisson* of nervous excitement – not to say barely concealed aggression – somehow contained within the rules of some arcane, unspoken ritual.

In an open area at the centre of this scene, a contest was taking place between two men who were wearing partial body armour and were armed with claymores. The contest constituted a savage series of swings and lunges, countered and returned with equally matched vehemence.

Watching from the side was a tall, broad-shouldered man with a strong ruthless face and shrewd eyes. One of the combatants was his man, and he urged him on in a low, intense voice, partisan but perceptive. This was the host – if that was the correct word – of the gathering: John Campbell, Duke of Argyll.

As the bout drew to its climax, Argyll's champion mounted a relentless series of attacks which drove his opponent back, defending desperately, and another figure drew closer to the combat. Slender, almost wizened with a masked, malevolent air about him, James Graham, Marquis of Montrose, was close to Argyll in age but in almost every other particular he was his opposite. From his exquisite wig to his elegant clothing he showed every sign of being a salon animal and his presence here seemed out of place, although he betrayed no discomfort in the rank, heated atmosphere. One thing was certain, however – the two men did not like each other.

With Montrose was a younger man, almost equally well dressed but with more of an air of the fop about him. His face, long and handsome in a slightly close-eyed, foxy fashion, betrayed an almost open contempt for the spectacle he was witnessing. He glanced occasionally at the contestants, but his eyes mainly roved over the scattering of women on display.

With a shout from the watchers the bout ended. Argyll's man had beaten his opponent literally to his knees, although the downed man was still desperately attempting to defend himself. A call came in from the side, and the defeated man at last gratefully conceded, slumping bruised, bleeding – and totally exhausted.

Argyll applauded the outcome, and as the crowd began to pay its gaming debts, Montrose and his companion moved over to join him. Argyll saw them and laughed.

'Montrose! Come hotfoot from Court to the cockpit . . . eh?'

Getting no reply, Argyll then turned his attention to Cunningham and eyed him up and down, seemingly assessing his function. Montrose, seeing this, introduced the younger man. 'May I present Archibald Cunningham . . . His Grace, the Duke of Argyll.'

Cunningham bowed. 'I am Your Grace's humble servant.'

Argyll acknowledged this with a curt nod, then, turning to Montrose with a smirk and a wicked glint in his perceptive eye, inquired of him: 'Another of your likely lads . . . ?'

'Archibald is sent me by his mother in the hope that our climate will cool the fever in his blood.'

Argyll looked Cunningham over, taking in the garb, the manner, the whole aura of the dandy. When he eventually did speak to Cunningham he conveyed a sense of utter and impregnable authority. It was the manner of a man who knew that he could say or do just about anything he liked without any consequence to himself whatsoever.

'So, Mr Cunningham, what are these principal sins that distress your mother . . . dice, drink, whores . . . ?' And the malice gleamed in his eye as he went on, '. . . Or are you a buggerer of boys?'

Cunningham smiled at the thrust. 'It is years, Your Grace, since I last buggered a boy – and in my own defence I must add I thought him a girl at the moment of entry.'

Argyll's swordsman had come up by now and stood listening, a raw-boned man with the look of a vicious dog.

Having set this up, Montrose, his eyes cold and missing nothing, watched from behind the mask of a barely interested manner. As he watched, his fingers played with the curls of his wig, twisting them idly, while his glance occasionally flickered over the ranks of faces and their gathering interest.

Argyll grinned at Cunningham's riposte, but unwilling to let it pass, carried on relentlessly and turned to his man. 'What say you, Guthrie, that Archie here could not tell arse from quim?'

'I have heard that many Englishmen have that difficulty.'

Argyll was delighted and slapped Guthrie on the shoulder. 'Spoken as well as you fought!'

Argyll turned to Cunningham, 'Did you see Guthrie

here at work, Mr Cunningham? Is he not a veritable Hector?'

'He is a fair hand with a cleaver, it must be said,' Cunningham responded disdainfully.

This jibe pleased Argyll, even more so as he sniffed the hint of further conflict. 'You don't think much of our Highland tools, then . . . ?'

'If I had to kill an ox, a claymore would be my first choice, Your Grace.'

Guthrie realized his expected role in the banter and was readily drawn into it. He reached out, took a hold of Cunningham's upper arm and squeezed it deprecatingly, 'Best use a musket and save the beast a slow dying, then.'

Cunningham looked askance at this counterpart of himself, every manner of recognition in his eyes. 'I would not need a musket for you, Guthrie.'

Argyll was delighted. Clapping his hands in delight, he looked at Montrose. 'I'll wager a hundred of what you like on Guthrie and his cleaver.'

Montrose stared back, poker-faced. 'At odds . . . ?'

'You are a fox, James. What odds?'

'Three.'

'Two.'

Montrose pressed on. 'English pounds?'

'Come, James, there's more of a jingle to guineas.'

'Guineas it is.'

Argyll was well satisfied and more than confident. 'Done. And the tools for your peacock? No, let me guess.' He looked Cunningham up and down again, and the look was one of pure malice. He continued: 'Rapier and poniard, in the Italian style . . . ?'

Cunningham nodded. 'Your Grace has an eye for character.'

'And I know yours to your teeth, lad,' and turning to Guthrie, Argyll continued, 'will you use a targe?'

Guthrie shook his head, his eyes never leaving Cunningham. 'No need, Your Grace.'

Argyll was even more jubilant. 'Excellent, excellent.'

He clapped his hands and a servant materialized. 'A bumper of Rhenish for my Lord Montrose and myself, and show Mr Cunningham what blades we have.'

Betting was now taking place all around the hall as Cunningham went to inspect the sword case and Guthrie retrieved his claymore and started to limber up. Montrose was watching all of this with his basilisk stare, fingers curled in the strands of his wig. Argyll, delighted with himself, went and fetched the two cups of wine and brought them back, handing one to Montrose.

Montrose accepted it with mock civility. 'You honour me, sir, to serve me with your own hand,' thinly disguised malice tainting his words.

Argyll laughed, enjoying the upper hand which he felt he now had over Montrose. 'I tell you, James, I forget how much you dislike me until I am in your presence. Then it rises from you like incense.' He took a long draught from his cup and relished it deeply. 'So what news at Court?'

Montrose shrugged and turned his back on the area where the contest was about to be held. 'What else but the succession? Our poor Queen cannot find time to die in peace. I fear she may pass over and leave the matter unresolved.'

The other man shook his head and mused, 'Would that she had seen a child of hers live to comfort the kingdom.'

On this broad sentiment at least the two of them could agree, and Montrose concurred icily, 'Aye. One might have hoped a field so regularly ploughed might have yielded one good crop. In truth I have seen healthier graveyards than that woman's womb.'

Cunningham and Guthrie were now confronting each other, and still all appearances indicated that Argyll's bet was the safer, as Cunningham took his stand with his faintly effete air, facing the big, dark-haired animal of a man that was Guthrie. Argyll was now fixed on the two men but Montrose, displaying a characteristically icy control, still had his back to the contestants, indicating his disdain for the mere mechanics of his conflict with Argyll. As if to hammer home the point he continued speaking, well aware that he was distracting the other.

'Now all watch to see which way to jump. You cannot go to the closet but that some adherent of James is praising your pish or one of George's men complimenting your stool.'

The contest began and almost from the outset, to everyone's surprise, it was patently evident that Guthrie was completely outclassed. Cunningham's earlier languor turned almost seamlessly into a supple, steely balance and he was moving around the heavier man in a series of smooth, fluent steps, his rapier flicking out, keeping Guthrie off balance and at bay, until in frustration the Highlander charged, swinging wildly. Then Cunningham with surprising calm moved inside, and shifting weapons between hands in a blur of speed, slashed Guthrie lightly across the midriff, hissing in his ear as he did so the one word, 'gutted'.

During this, Montrose, still with his back to these events, continued his own slashing, probing talk which Argyll was only slowly coming to recognize as the verbal equivalent of what he was watching happen to his champion on the floor.

He went on: 'I confess to a certain weariness upon the whole issue, and look to the likes of Your Grace to give some lead. Where Argyll goes the path must be broad and firm, and I have an aversion to getting my feet mired in such matters.'

Cunningham now pressed home his attack, his slender, almost delicate weapon making a series of lightning flicks and slashes so that the Highlander began to bleed from a series of savage little cuts.

And now Montrose likewise went on the attack, and, as if unconsciously anticipating the works of Adam Smith by about fifty years or so, somewhat pompously averred: 'I am asked continually on which side Your Grace will declare himself. All I could answer in honesty was that it would be the one which was most inclined to his own benefit, for if there is a higher principle than enlightened self-interest, I am yet to have it explained to me.'

Argyll, realizing from the spectacle before him that he had been set up and was now being taunted, suddenly snapped and, all pretence of *bonhomie* gone, snarled, 'Dammit man, but you talk too much. Can you not tend to your wager?'

And Montrose's satisfaction was complete, betraying itself only in the thinnest of smiles, 'Ach, Argyll, my wager is well won.'

Montrose at last turned to the floor where Cunningham had moved from baiting to closure and was manœuvring Guthrie back, both hands brilliantly at work, forcing the Highlander to use his claymore for defence, driving him until he was almost brought to where Argyll and Montrose stood. Then Cunningham deftly feinted with the sword and went in with the poniard, taking Guthrie under the chin, lifting his head high till it seemed that he carried it on the point.

He looked into Guthrie's eyes. 'Be grateful our masters wagered money and not lives.' And he increased the pressure until the point pierced the skin and blood dribbled down the blade. Then, with a swift step back, Cunningham bowed to his helpless adversary and, as applause broke out from the spectators, he turned his back on Guthrie and took a further bow.

Guthrie was seized with rage. His arm came up and he began to make at his tormentor's back. Cunningham would have been a dead man had it not been for Argyll's voice, angry and imperative, halting the Highlander.

'Dammit, Guthrie, is it not enough that you are beaten, but you must turn back-stabber . . .'

Argyll stormed out, his servants following, and with Guthrie, suddenly hangdog, taking up the rear. Cunningham watched him go as Montrose called after the departing retinue: 'I will have my factor call on Your Grace's factor.'

CHAPTER THREE

Better to Virginia than to starve

> *Yet was Rob Roy as* wise *as brave;*
> *Forgive me if the phrase be strong;*
> *A poet worthy of Rob Roy*
> *Must turn a timid song.*

It was early morning, and Rob and the others had already been travelling for some hours. They were driving Montrose's recovered cattle down the heather and bracken of the hillside above a small *clachan* of two dozen or so low cottages. These were primitive dwellings, built of unmortared dry-stone walls with sods of turf for roofing, and mostly without the benefit of windows or chimneys – unpretentious but sturdy.

As they approached the dwellings, doors opened and people came out to greet them. Obviously glad to see the safe arrival of the drovers, the inhabitants took over the task of corralling the beasts as Rob and the others fell out to take their ease. They were exhausted and hard-marked by the drive, and they took such sustenance as their families brought them with relief as they gratefully dropped down to rest against the cottage walls.

Rob was weary in spirit as well as in body. As he looked around at the scene, his eyes were flickering across the tired faces of the old and the young alike and a shadow of concern set into his face. McDonald came over to him with a jug. They did not speak as Rob took it and cradled it in his arm while he drank. McDonald was watching carefully as Rob slowly handed the jug back. Eventually their eyes met when Rob looked up and sighed with resignation.

'Cut out another of the cattle. If the tinkers ate one, they could have eaten two.'

McDonald was uneasy. 'Montrose will charge you, none the less.'

'I'm weary of seeing children hungry and old folk cold,' came the oblique reply.

'It'll take more than a cow to fix that, Rob.'

Rob stared at him, angry at this. 'Aye, well, you'll be in the Americas living off the fat, so it won't be worrying you.'

McDonald was hurt and was more than ready to defend himself, but then Coll came out to them from inside the house they had been sitting against. There was a woman behind him, carrying a dish of hot, steaming liquid.

'Have some broth, Rob, fresh off the fire.'

Rob shook his head. 'No, Coll, I'm for home.'

But Coll's wife dipped a piece of bread into the stew and handed it to him. Rob took it and gestured with it to her.

'Your kindness, Morag . . .'

Her reply was heartfelt, 'And yours, Rob. God bless you.'

After this briefest of repasts, Rob walked wearily down through the houses, quietly exchanging greetings with the people, and went on along towards a path which angled away across the hillside into the already thickening dark . . .

Meanwhile Alasdair had been recounting recent events, with breathless mime and considerable amplification, to a rapt band of admiring but somewhat disbelieving listeners.

'Then Rob just walks in among them, bold as a linnet, his sword still in its sheath, and says, "Waken up you bunch of ragged-arse tinker cow thieves". And there were a dozen and a half of them, at the very smallest count, all of them armed to the teeth and their leader a great brute of a tinker with teeth like a boar and a smell to match, and Rob goes up to him and says, "Tell your crew to lay down and I'll only cut *your* throat, else I'll call my men", and we're all there, ready for the word, "and not a one of you will breakfast in this world".'

Pausing for effect, which, to a degree, he attained, he continued: 'Well, that put a bee in his bum, I can tell you, and he didn't know whether to scratch his arse or blow it away with a fart.'

In the dusk, McDonald, breathless and uneasy, caught up with Rob and fell in alongside him. 'I would not have you go off in an ill frame of mind with me, Rob. I meant no harm . . .'

Conscious of his own weariness and the short temper that it might have brought about, Rob acknowledged this apology with gentleness. 'Pay me no heed. My mouth spoke before I gave it leave. But you and your Americas, they're not for me.'

The proprieties satisfied, McDonald, however, was not quite ready to let the tenor of this matter drop. 'Better to Virginia than to starve; and another winter like the last will see a boatload of that.'

This insistence was ill-judged, for it served only to rekindle Rob's ire. 'These are my blood-kin and this is my country. You are a free agent, Alan, and may starve where you please.'

Nettled, McDonald felt justified in once again venting his anger. 'I am as much kin to you as any. It's not blood alone that makes bonds. You told me long since ever to speak my mind to you. Well, these are hard times – getting harder.'

During this, Rob, seeing the truth of it, softened, and his expression moved from annoyance to the affection of respect and kinship. He put a hand on McDonald's shoulder.

'Aye, that they are, and I am taking thought for them.

But you do well to goad me, for, left to myself, I'm a lazy horse.'

And McDonald was instantly remorseful, his regard for the man next to him overwhelming, shaking his head he gently quipped: 'And I'm the next King of Scotland.'

Rob suddenly laughed uproariously. 'God spare you such a fate!' In a sense, they could share common ground in this joke, and McDonald appreciated the concession.

They embraced and went their predetermined ways – Rob to Craigrostan and McDonald, after a moment, slowly turned and headed back towards the *clachan*, where Alasdair, inevitably, was still regaling the group of children – joined now by some of the men who didn't have the good fortune to nurture a share in the glory of having been on the foray . . .

CHAPTER FOUR

At Craigrostan House

Say, then, that he was wise as brave;
As wise in thought as bold in deed:
For in the principles of things
He *sought his moral creed.*

The loch was a flat calm. In the cool of the morning ghostly wisps of pearly white mist floated a few feet above the dark surface of the water. Rob was standing in it, naked, sluicing himself down and relishing the chill waters. He was suddenly aware of a whimpering behind him and turned round.

The dog was at the water's edge, eager to join him but reluctant to plunge into the loch. Behind the dog, some fifty yards back on a shelving spit of land, was a low but substantial stone house with a few outbuildings. It squatted dourly in the grey morning light, silent and unlit.

Rob came wading back to the shore, greeted the dog by tousling its ears, and picked up his clothes. Roughly drying himself off he walked slowly back to the house.

Inside the house there were two main areas divided by a simple partition. In the larger area there were two children asleep on palliasses – boys of seven and nine. In the other room a woman was in bed on a raised platform, her face turned to the wall. She did not stir as Rob came in, laid down his clothes and gear and went back over to the bed. He raised the bedclothes, breathed in the aroma of wife and home, and slipped in naked and damp beside her.

The chill of him suddenly reached her, and she shivered and turned round to face him, still asleep. She had a strong, handsome face, with dark brown hair, tumbling around her shoulders. Rob held her. She smiled and murmured, her eyes still closed. 'I dreamed a silkie came.'

His palms, still as loch-cold as a fish, were already under her shift. She shivered and smiled as he said, wet beard against her ear, 'And what did he do with you – your silkie . . . ?'

She smiled a drugged, slack smile of sleep, eyes still closed. 'You wakened me before the best of it.'

And she turned into his embrace, her mouth drinking his neck, 'But he would have ravished me for certain.'

They kissed, hot and cold, and, after their lips had

parted, Rob said whimsically, 'How do you know you are awake, wife?'

She smiled and returned to the submarine world where all was possible, and Rob, gently, but with the assurance of one who knew his way, turned her on her back, and lying beside her at a right angle, legs beneath her raised knees, he sought and entered her – a slow, yielding thrust that caused the smile on her face to expand slowly in wonder and delight.

On the glass of the loch's surface a fish rose, and a ring of ripples broke and spread in a slow silken circle.

Later, Rob and Mary were walking slowly but steadily up the hill above the lochside. The boys, Duncan and Ranald, were running ahead with the dog. Mary was carrying a basket on her arm. Her walk was an easy, lithe one with a long, outdoor stride.

Quietly Rob said, 'I killed Tam Sibbald yesterday morning.'

Mary looked at him sharply. Rob was thinking back on the event, his face grave.

He continued. 'We played at the ball once, at Crieff market . . . I remember shouting, "Well done, Tam!" when he made a run.'

Rob, whose eyes had been fixed firmly ahead, now looked back at her in return. 'And there he was, hung on the end of my dirk like meat.'

She handed him the basket in a matter-of-fact attempt to break his mood and said, 'Aye, well, likely it was necessary.'

Rob shook his head. 'Aye, it was necessary enough to save worse. But them tinkers ... they were not all broken men, Mary. Some of them had kin and clans. They made me fear I might have come across one of our own among them.'

'McGregors are not tinkers.'

Rob sighed, 'I think we are but a hard winter or two away, some of us . . .'

She took his arm, 'What's gnawing on you, Robert? Speak it out.'

He stopped, and it was plain that he had given this matter much thought. 'I have made my mind to borrowing money from Montrose to buy cattle at Crieff market and sell at Carlisle.' Mary's silence simply made Rob continue with more force: 'Believe me, Mary, this will turn profit. Six pound in Crieff's, twelve in Carlisle.'

'How much money?'

'A thousand pound.'

Mary was shocked and merely stared at him in disbelief.

'I know cattle, Mary, and I can drive them faster and deliver them fatter than any man in the kingdom.'

'And why should the Marquis of Montrose lend a McGregor a thousand pound?' This was spoken in a tone with more than a hint of incredulity.

'For profit, what else? It would be investment as much as a loan.'

If he had hoped to convince her with this, her reply was quickly to disillusion him. 'Oh, it's business partners you are now, you and the Marquis . . . ?'

Rob flushed with anger. 'Keep that tongue for your weans, woman. I did not tell you my mind to be flayed for it.' He swung away, and started up the hill to where the boys and the dog had stopped in the middle of a circle of standing stones.

Mary watched him for a moment, rueful rather than contrite. After a moment she ran after him, caught his arm and fell into step beside him. 'I love the bones of you, Robert McGregor, but you take too much to heart that cannot be helped.'

Rob didn't look at her but merely said, 'It *must* be helped.'

'All right, but not today, eh?'

He looked down at her, and she up at him. A kind of unspoken truce passed between them and they walked on, joined at the hip.

They settled down with the boys and after they had all eaten, Rob, his back to one of the stones with Duncan and Ranald on each side, gestured at the stones and became reflective. Mary was watching from a little way off, stroking the dog's head in her lap.

'Our blood goes back to the kings of Scotland, the McAlpines, beyond all reckoning and back to these . . .' He pointed at the stones. 'The olden folk who raised these stones and knew these hills as we do.'

Duncan thought about this for a moment and then asked rather wistfully, 'Will McGregors ever be kings again?'

Rob laughed a long, warm, generous laugh, and placing a broad palm on the heads of his two sons proclaimed, 'I crown you kings of the hill, and lords of the stones.'

Ranald, not satisfied, insisted: 'No, but will we . . . ?'

Rob looked at the bright, questing face of the boy and replied somewhat inscrutably, 'All men with honour are kings, but not all kings have honour.'

Duncan, not satisfied by any of this, asked: 'What is honour?'

'Honour is what no man can give you and none can take away. Honour is a man's gift to himself.' Mary was still looking on, her face keenly showing the affection she felt for the three of them as Duncan asked:

'Do women have it?'

Mary laughed at this but Rob continued seriously.

'Women are the heart of honour, and we cherish and protect it in them. You must never mistreat a woman or malign a man, nor stand by and see another do so,' Rob replied with some feeling.

'How do you know if you have it?' Ranald insisted.

'Never worry on the getting of it. It grows in you and speaks to you . . . all you need do is listen.'

This deeply held certainty touched Mary, and she lowered her eyes and rubbed the dog's muzzle to express the emotions the man aroused in her. Rob tousled the boys' hair roughly.

'All right lads, enough of the finer things. You have beasts to tend to and water to haul. Away with you.'

The boys got up and the dog jumped up with them, eager for the off. Mary stirred as if to join them. But Rob continued, 'Your mother and me will be down directly.'

And Mary settled back, sidelong in the grass, and said only, 'Take the basket.'

The boys picked it up and started to run pell-mell down the slope, yelling with the sheer exuberance of the day. Rob and Mary remained, yards apart, and looked at each other silently for a long moment.

Finally, it was Rob who broke the silence. 'Do you know how fine you are to me, Mary McGregor? So fine.'

Mary moved across to him and settled between his knees. He took her head between his hands and murmured again, 'So fine . . .'

They kissed; a long, sensuous, mouth-melding moment. Mary eventually pulled herself back and asked, 'Is that why you sent them away, to tell me how fine I am?'

Her hands went slowly between his legs, gentle and certain. Rob looked at her in mock surprise as she continued teasingly, 'Or did you want to make a silk purse out of my sow's ear again . . . ?'

Rob smiled. 'What a wanton I am wed on.'

Her body rose up between his knees, her mouth close to his ear as she whispered, 'You know what the old wives say about these standing stones?'

'No, what do the old wives say, old wife?'

She squeezed him hard enough to make him cry out, laughing, 'No, no, tell me, what do they say?'

She pulled herself up and settled down on him, guiding his already strong erection inside.

'They say that the stones make men hard and women fertile.'

They were now firmly joined, and then Rob, with a

strong and sudden upthrust, impaled her more deeply. She shuddered against him and her eyes closed, as Rob said softly: 'I think we have no need of them, you and me.'

She opened her eyes and looked down on him, love and lust perfectly fused in equal balance in her face. 'Do you know how fine you are to me, Robert McGregor?'

His only reply was with his body, which rocked up under her like a bucking horse or a breaking wave. A cloud passed like a great dark quilt over their oblivious bodies.

CHAPTER FIVE

This country does not agree with me

Said generous Rob, 'What need of books?
Burn all the statutes and their shelves:
They stir us up against our kind;
And worse, against ourselves.'

Outside Montrose's house, which was as well tended and reeking of new money as Argyll's was run-down and shabby, a figure came hurrying down the path towards the small coach-house at the far end of the grounds. He was a big and burly, and yet at the same time, skittish man who bustled along with short, busy strides.

Within the coach-house was Cunningham's bedroom. It was a low-ceilinged room with small deep-set windows. Most of the room was taken up by a huge bed. In the bed Cunningham lay asleep with his nightshirt twisted about him, his hair damp on his head with perspiration.

A young woman was at the foot of the bed, getting dressed. Betty was struggling into her clothing, which along with her demeanour conveyed her status as that of a servant. She was pretty and plump and concerned about her girth – and, just for this precise moment, about not waking the man. She took one love-lorn look at him, examined herself in the looking-glass which was so amply convex as to make any accurate assessment impossible, then made quickly for the door.

As she opened it she found the burly figure of a man standing outside, as if he had been there a week. She reacted in a panic of recognition. 'Mr Killearn . . . I'm on my way . . .'

Killearn blocked her exit and smiled, his eyes bright with malice and more.

'*Well* on the way, I'd venture . . .'

As she tried to get past him he pressed his belly against her, causing her to struggle.

'Let me be, Mr Killearn. You'll wake him. Don't! Mr Killearn.' This exclamation was made as she felt a hand suddenly thrust under her skirt.

'I'm sure the young master keeps you nicely greased, does he not?' His hand, even more insistent than his jocular tone, went between her legs, and he smiled at the accuracy of his prediction.

'You'd hardly feel me going in, Betty.'

The girl struggled, desperate to free herself but equally somehow to keep quiet at the same time.

Meanwhile, she could hear that behind her, Cunningham was starting to stir, and, with a little cry, she wrenched herself free, partly by her own efforts, partly by dint of Killearn's relinquishing of his hold – and she was out and away.

Killearn came over to look down on the face of the man in the bed. In his eyes there was a look of fathomless, amused contempt. He held the fingers of the hand he had had between Betty's legs under Cunningham's nose.

'A wee whiff o' quim in the morning, Mr Cunningham? Just the thing to clear your head.'

It must have had some revivifying effect for, indeed, Cunningham's features slowly reacted. His eyelids fluttered upwards, as if recovering from a faint, and Killearn smiled.

Cunningham certainly did begin to come awake. His eyes were now open and he looked up. By now Killearn had his hand behind his back, and his sober face was on for this – his voice unctuous with self-abasement.

'Mr Cunningham . . . I hope I'm not disturbing you.'

Cunningham jerked himself up against the headboard, instantly irritable, and angrily stated the obvious.

'Of course you're bloody well disturbing me.' He rubbed his face as if trying to rearrange his features. 'Do you think I want to wake up and see some great smelly Scotchman standing over me?'

He threw his legs out of the bed, hooked a chamber pot from beneath it, and proceeded to pee into it with careless relief.

'What are you doing here?'

Killearn moved himself round the bed as if to afford himself a better view. 'I wanted to tell you that some of the local tradesfolk have been pressing for payment on your debt.'

Cunningham stared at him, amazed and annoyed at the same time.

'And you woke me to tell me that?'

'A thousand apologies to you, Mr Cunningham, but they have also writ to His Lordship.'

This cut off the pee in mid-stream – an effect greatly appreciated by Cunningham's tormentor.

'Dammit, man, I but recently earned His Lordship two hundred guineas. What are the complaints of a few tradesmen to such services?'

He got up, vainly affecting indifference, and kicked the chamber pot back as he walked around the bed. Killearn, unfooled, watched him, self-satisfied malice oozing out of his eyes.

Cunningham stood in front of the bulging looking-glass. As he tried to adjust his focus he suddenly became unhappy about his increasingly dissolute appearance. He contrived to catch a glimpse of Killearn, who, just at the right moment, had managed to go blank-faced. Cunningham caught and held Killearn's eye for an instant, then, staring, managed briefly to reconstruct an image of his own face again.

'This country does not agree with me. I cannot wait until I am out of the damnable place.'

'The sentiments of a great many of us, Mr Cunningham.'

Killearn continued in his unctuous fashion. 'Would you like me to remove your chamber pot?'

Cunningham, thrown by this, merely stared. Killearn took his silence as acquiescence. He went round and retrieved the vessel, without betraying a trace of revulsion. As he passed Cunningham he proclaimed, the very soul of *gravitas*, 'I know of many a Scotsman who would be glad of a dram of this on a cold morning. It's almost pure spirit – or I'm no judge of a pint of pish.'

Chapter Six

To know one's place

'We have a passion – make a law,
Too false to guide us or control!
And for the law itself we fight
In bitterness of soul.'

In a fashionably high-vaulted and elegantly proportioned room, Montrose was furiously waving a fistful of papers in Cunningham's face. A few paces away, Killearn, leaning against the wall, was practising the subtle arts of invisibility.

Montrose was almost screaming in his incredulity: 'And this tailor in Glasgow to whom you owe eighty-seven pounds extended this credit because you were my guest? Or, as you preferred to frame it, "a member of my household".'

Cunningham was uneasily trying to defuse the

situation, but with not much success. 'I can assure His Lordship I have in no manner indebted him.'

Montrose was totally unmollified and continued, 'And now Killearn tells me you are saddling one of my serving wenches.' At this Cunningham turned to glare at Killearn, who steadfastly contrived to stare straight ahead while Montrose continued, 'Dammit, man, your mother did not send you to me to debauch innocent girls.'

'I regret that I have so offended Your Lordship. By your leave I will remove myself.'

Montrose stared at him amazed, and continued vindictively, 'And to where, might I ask? You are penniless. You have no mount. You know no one. To where will you remove yourself?'

Before Cunningham had the chance to reply, Montrose pushed home his advantage and spat at him, 'Have you some notion of presenting yourself at the Duke of Argyll's door, soliciting his patronage as his new champion?'

Montrose saw that he was not so far off the mark as Cunningham bowed his head. 'I am Your Lordship's to command.'

Montrose stood for a long, malevolent moment before concluding the matter. 'Remember your place, sir. That is all I ask of any man.'

He turned away to address Killearn, leaving Cunningham white-faced and shaken. 'What is next?'

'McGregor, my Lord,' Killearn replied.

Montrose stood for a moment as if he was trying to

recall what or who McGregor was. Then, abruptly to Cunningham, 'You may go, Archibald.'

Cunningham bowed and took his leave. As he exited into the hall every sinew was trembling with anger. He strode down the hall to recover his sword and scabbard from the bench, and passed the waiting Rob Roy without a glance.

Killearn waited to let Cunningham get clear and then, looking out at the attendant McGregor, asked cautiously:

'You bear no arms?'

'I had not planned to insist terms at sword-point,' Rob replied quietly.

Killearn pressed on portentously, 'It is against all usage for someone of your station to enter a nobleman's presence bearing arms.' He took Rob's arm and officiously bustled him towards the door, looking backward to reassure himself that Cunningham was well out of the way. 'When His Lordship speaks, do not presume to interject until he gives you leave.'

As they entered the room, Montrose was at the far end staring gloomily down on to his gardens. He looked round as Killearn led Rob up.

'Robert McGregor of Craigrostan, Your Lordship.'

Montrose turned and took a pace towards them. 'I knew your father, McGregor. An able man, if not a wise one. Have you taken on his mantle?'

'As best I may, Your Lordship.'

Montrose studied him for a moment before asking in

his sardonic style, 'So, you are the master of how many men . . . ?'

'Master of none, Your Lordship, but some two hundred souls are close by Craigrostan and in my care.'

'And you are prophet and provider to them – is it not so?'

Rob was nettled by Montrose's hectoring tone, but shrugged and replied, 'What I can, I do. It is no great matter compared to Your Lordship's world.'

Montrose smiled. 'Ah, McGregor, to know one's place in the order of things is a great blessing.' He turned towards Killearn, all at once as dry as an abacus, 'What terms, Killearn?'

Just as aridly Killearn snapped back, 'A fifth of the principal within three month, Your Lordship.'

'A fifth, you say? Is this fellow your kin that you propose him such kindly terms? Am I not accustomed to a quarter on unsecured loans?'

'McGregor has three hundred acres at Craigrostan, Your Lordship.'

Montrose turned to Rob and calmly surveyed him. 'A man of property, intent on growing richer? We have more in common than I would have suspected, McGregor.'

Rob remained silent, ill liking this comparison. Montrose continued. 'So, a thousand pound for three month and these acres of yours as security?'

'And my oath . . .'

Montrose's eyes flickered. 'Ah, yes. Tell me, McGregor, is there anything to what Killearn says – that you might have run off my cattle and then returned them with tales of tinkers caught and summarily executed?'

Rob glanced angrily but uncertainly at Killearn, who had temporarily found a cornice of great interest to investigate at the far end of the room. After a pause Rob replied, 'I have, in my day, reived cattle, Your Lordship, but none that were under my watch.'

Montrose smiled and pushed his advantage home. 'Is that what passes for honour with a McGregor, then . . . ?'

Rob stiffened under this gratuitous insult but replied, 'What passes for honour with me is likely enough the same as with Your Lordship. When my word is given, it is good.'

Montrose was now becoming bored with this baiting and turning away quipped, 'You are to be congratulated on such cheaply bought nobility. Killearn will draw papers and I will expect the terms to be met.'

Rob realized that the interview was at an end and inclined his head. 'My thanks to Your Lordship.'

Silently, Killearn ushered him out.

CHAPTER SEVEN

Sheep-shaggers the lot of you

'And, puzzled, blinded thus, we lose
Distinctions that are plain and few:
These find I graven on my heart:
That *tells me what to do.'*

The tavern where the contract was to be concluded was a mean, low-ceilinged affair, thick with smoke and the sweaty stench of intoxicated bodies. Rob and McDonald were seated with Killearn at a low table against the wall. Rob had signed the document and passed it over to Killearn, who dusted the paper with sand and held it up to blow it dry.

'It's a fine, bold signature you have – worthy of a chieftain.'

A boy brought up their drinks and stared at Rob. 'Are you Rob Roy McGregor?'

Rob looked at him and nodded. 'I am. And what is your name?'

The boy quickly replied, 'Davie Anderson', before darting away into the throng. Killearn raised his drink and mockingly commented, 'Even the serving boys know you. You've become a famous reiver and retriever in your own life.'

Uneasily, Rob and McDonald exchanged glances as Killearn sarcastically toasted them, 'To business and profit.'

Rob added in a whisper, 'And a soft winter,' as they raised their glasses and drank.

Suddenly they became aware of an intruder at their table. He had the thick belligerent glare of the drunken quarreller spoiling to pick a fight. It was Argyll's champion, Guthrie. Looking directly at Rob he echoed the boy's words and asked accusingly, 'Are you Rob Roy McGregor?'

'I am.'

'I am Will Guthrie. Have you heard of me?'

Rob replied in all honesty, 'I have not.'

Guthrie glared back. 'Well, I have heard of you.'

And the tavern began to fall silent as the assembled company sensed the opening rounds of a confrontation. Rob met Guthrie's eyes. 'Indeed. And what have you heard, Mr Guthrie?'

'That you back-stabbed Tam Sibbald.'

The room was hushed now. Rob did not hurry, but sat impassive and poker-faced for a moment before asking, 'Were you kin to Tam?'

'Near enough. I shagged his sister,' replied Guthrie.

Rather unwisely, Killearn could not resist the opening. 'Likely so did Tam . . .'

But there was no laugh from the audience, and the remark fell flat as Guthrie, with a speed which belied his drunken state, drew his sword and had it at Killearn's throat, forcing the latter against the wall.

'You want the wind let out your bladder?' Killearn, suddenly more circumspect, had no clever riposte to this question and it was Rob who responded.

'What is your business with me, Guthrie?'

Guthrie slowly and disgustedly removed his attention from Killearn and turned to address Rob.

'Business best done outside.' And Guthrie rested the blade on the table with the edge up and the point directed straight at Rob's chest.

'We have no quarrel,' Rob observed.

'That can be remedied.'

The tavern was now totally silent and paralysed in a many-eyed expectancy of the by now inevitable. McDonald's hand crept slowly and instinctively to the *skian dhu* sheathed in the top of his hose. The boy who had inadvertently brought all of this to pass by the mention of Rob's name stared on in disbelief. Killearn, trying once again to become invisible, slid slowly down the bench, never letting the upturned blade out of his sight.

Rob seemed to be almost savouring the moment and allowed it to drag out. Then, almost as if making terms, challenged, 'To the first cut.'

Guthrie nodded. But almost before his head had stopped moving, Rob had stolen the initiative by sweeping his palm across the edge of the blade which was still resting on the table, drawing blood, and holding it up to Guthrie and the whole tavern. 'Well done!'

There was a moment's silence before the entire company erupted in laughter and applause. Guthrie was confused and furious. In the next instant Rob was round from behind the table and at Guthrie's side, looking him straight in the eye.

'Some other time when we are both sober.'

Rob winked at the serving boy who was staring at him in awe, and strode out of the tavern before Guthrie had the chance to respond. Guthrie was nonplussed, and stood staring for a moment before lurching heavily back to the counter as the tavern reverted to its normal buzzing conversation. McDonald got up and quickly followed Rob out while Killearn stared daggers at his exiting back.

Rob was untying his plaid from the saddle of a small, wiry horse as McDonald came up to join him. Rob gave him a look and a short shake of the head, which conveyed relief and exasperation.

'That Sibbald has a longer reach dead than he ever did living. I'm away home. Keep the pony, and stick to Killearn till you have the note. I'll see you at Craigrostan.'

McDonald took Rob's hand and examined it before nodding his agreement. Rob wrapped his plaid around him before trudging off into the night. McDonald watched him go for a moment, stroking the horse's neck, before turning back into the tavern.

The company had relaxed back into humdrum normality and McDonald rejoined Killearn, who was downing a large aquavit in a generally successful attempt to recover his composure. Killearn looked expectantly at McDonald, who responded to his glance, 'I am to wait here till the note is signed.'

Killearn had now more or less recovered and decided to make this clear by needling McDonald. 'My but you're the obedient one. Fetch and carry at command. Tell me, McDonald, why has a smart young lad like yourself attached himself to such a crew? I would have thought you more fit to serve a man like my master, the Marquis of Montrose.'

McDonald, his pride touched, would have none of this, and said without a hint of deference and with some care and composure, 'I dare say your master is a great man in matters of this world, Killearn. But I'd lay his soul in the scale, and throw in a dozen of yours for makeweight, and watch it tip Rob's way every time.'

Killearn was infuriated and allowed himself to be provoked into an outburst. 'God! But what a crew you are, you Highlanders with your airs and honours – you come begging a thousand pound as if you were doing the lender a favour . . . Sheep-shaggers, the lot of you!'

The insult failed to make its mark as McDonald was already taking his leave. Smiling to himself, Killearn then made a low 'baa-ing' sound which in its controlled derision drew gales of laughter from the watching company that McDonald affected not to hear. Killearn, endeavouring to recover himself, drew in a deep breath and sat staring balefully and malevolently at the wall in front of him.

Chapter Eight

At a fair price . . .

'The creatures see of flood and field,
And those that travel on the wind!
With them no strife can last; they live
In peace, and peace of mind.'

In his room at Montrose's house, Cunningham and Betty were in bed. It was the middle of the night and he was pleasantly and satisfactorily drunk – a deep, almost calm intoxication on which his mind floated like a cork rising and falling on a gentle swell. For her part, Betty was also in her own way just as inebriated, but purely on the heady spirit of post-coital proximity to her beloved.

Betty was examining a painted miniature of the idealized head and shoulders of a lady who betrayed all of the conventionalized features of beauty of the period. Meanwhile Cunningham was musing, half to Betty, half to himself, 'My mother could come no nearer than three candidates for my paternity. The Earl of Rutland – now there's a name for a whoremaster; a secretary to the Spanish ambassador, whose name she hazarded as Ferdinando; and some buck she never saw who raised her skirts at a masked ball.'

Betty was innocently shocked. 'He ravished her?'

Cunningham chuckled cynically and reached for the bottle. 'I would put it no higher than "surprised".'

He took a long swig and when he was at last done, Betty kissed his wet lips for her share. Then, greatly daring, she looked into his eyes.

'Archie, take me with you.'

Cunningham stared at her, his normal look of insolent irritation showing, but she persisted. 'Wherever, whatever, take me away with you.'

Cunningham was suddenly reflective and bitter. 'Away with me? I *am* "away", Betty, and God help me, this is where I've landed. You think me a gentleman because I have linen and can manage a lisp? I am but a bastard abroad, seeking my fortune and the favour of great men – as big a whore as my mother ever was . . .'

And then suddenly the truth of the matter burst forth from her in a tone of complete guilelessness.

'I am pregnant by you, Archie.'

Cunningham looked at her without rancour,

something close to acknowledgement of their equal plight in his eyes. He shook his head and put a hand to her face. 'Well, when he asks you for his father's name, at least you'll have it to give.'

Reassured by this tenderness she kissed him, and he kissed her back. Then, as if sent to destroy the moment, there was a knocking at the door followed by the voice of Killearn.

'Mr Cunningham . . . it is Killearn. A word with you.'

Betty shrank down in the bed and whispered, 'Don't let him see me.'

However, Cunningham was already up and furiously striding over to the door.

As Betty shrank further down beneath the bedding, Cunningham opened the door and gazed at the insipid smile which played around Killearn's lips. Enraged, Cunningham seized him by the throat in a vicious grip and, nearly throttling him, forced him to his knees. Killearn's eyes boggled as he gasped and choked, trying in vain to wrench the hand away. But Cunningham was, quite simply, too strong for him.

Her heart in her mouth, Betty risked a peek from beneath the covers. All she could see was Cunningham's strong back as Killearn struggled, gasping, to tear himself away by throwing himself backward on the landing. He lay there and stared up at Cunningham, who closed the door and stepped outside.

Betty, part horrified and part thrilled, sat up.

Unable to resist she got up and went to listen at the door.

Cunningham was staring at Killearn as the latter attempted to get up.

'You are a carbuncle on this arse of a country, Killearn, and if you ever inform against me to His Lordship again, I will squeeze the pus out of you with my bare hands.'

There was absolutely no doubt now in Killearn's mind that this vicious figure before him was perfectly willing and able to make good such a promise. Killearn steadied himself and massaged his throat and yet, curiously, there was little sign of fear in his voice as he made his sarcastic response.

'My, but you have a rare contempt in you, Archie.'

Cunningham bridled at this and took a step forward. Killearn backed away.

'I gave you no leave to call me familiar . . .' Cunningham hissed.

Killearn impudently asked, 'Could I pay for the privilege?'

Cunningham frowned at this as Killearn continued, '. . . At a fair price.'

'A fair price . . . ?'

Killearn replied, 'The easiest ever earned for a man of your parts.'

Cunningham showed his interest by stepping closer to Killearn who held his ground.

'What are you gibbering about?' Cunningham asked.

'Money, Archie, what else?'

Cunningham was sufficiently curious to let this second familiarity pass unheeded.

'How much money?'

Killearn, who realized his bait had taken, softly said, 'Let us go inside and talk over a dram. It's chill on the stairs . . .'

'Say what you have to say. I am engaged within.'

'Ah, you have Betty on her back?'

Cunningham ignored this with the question, 'How *much* money, man?'

Chapter Nine

To be repaid within three months at interest

'For why? – because the good old rule
Sufficeth them, the simple plan,
That they should take, who have the power,
And they should keep who can.'

At the centre of the handful of humble steadings that formed the heart of the *clachan*, the menfolk were gathered. Alasdair, Coll, Gregor and Iain were all focused on Rob and following his every word. At last a collective gasp rose to the surface of the conversation.

'A thousand pounds!'

Rob nodded. 'To be repaid within three month at interest.'

Alasdair was still disbelieving. 'A thousand pound . . . what does a thousand pound look like . . . ?' His hands spread wide. 'Will we have ponies enough to carry it?'

Rob explained. 'Not coin. A note of credit drawn on His Lordship.'

'At what interest, Rob?' Coll asked.

'A fifth,' came the reply, and there were whistles and more gasps.

Iain pointed out the obvious. 'He has two hundred pound profit in three month . . . ?'

Rob explained patiently, as if to children. 'It is the cost of cash and we must plan the matter to the last penny. When Alan returns he will take three of you and go to Crieff. There you will bargain with the drovers and have the herd assembled when I come with our kit for the drive.'

Gregor, out of his depth, was uncertain. 'How many, Rob? How big a herd?'

'Three hundred. Maybe more . . .'

There was a general buzz of excitement as Alasdair added, 'What a herd . . . and whatever we can acquire along the way.'

Rob grinned as he caught Alasdair's drift. 'No harm if a dozen or more stick.'

Coll was getting carried away already at the prospect of such glory. His eyes shone. 'We'll drive them into Carlisle like an army.'

Rob looked around at the eager, excited faces. 'So let us have all hands to it and we'll stay warm this winter – within and without – and to celebrate it, we'll hold a gathering and drink to our success.'

A shout went up at this, a shout of long-denied hope and of survival.

* * *

That evening the *ceilidh* was well under way. The whole *clachan* was out – a hundred people or more – and the music of the fiddle rinsed the air as the beat and clap of the dancers drifted out across the forested slopes of the lower part of the hillside. Below, Loch Lomond was still reflecting a salmon-pink light from the sky, although the far shore had long been deep in the shadow of Ben Vorlich and the peaks to the south of Loch Sloy.

A half-cow on a huge spit was glistening over the flames of a lively fire and the aquavit was circulating freely. The women were at their bagpipes while the dancers span faster and faster to the wild, exhausting pace of the reel and the jig.

Mary was dancing with Alasdair whose pace had more than a hint of the demonic about it. But he brought out the best in her, so that she seemed half her age as the music relentlessly urged them both on. The dance ended with a great whoop and Alasdair brought her back to where Rob was sitting before heading off in search of a fresh partner.

Mary sank down exhausted beside Rob. 'That Alasdair Roy is a fierce dancer.'

As she swept her hair back out of her eyes Rob leaned over against her and whispered into her ear, 'The last time I saw you in such a lather, you were flat on your back.'

Mary, pretending to be annoyed, elbowed him hard enough to make him grunt and scolded, 'Do not affront me afore folk.'

Coll, who was sitting close by, thought he caught the gist of what was going on and leaned over as Rob was pulling Mary closer. 'Do you know why Calvinists are against shagging standing up?'

Rob looked quizzically over at Mary, a whimsical smile playing around his mouth. Mary responded with eyes raised skyward and a look of mock exasperation which expressed quite clearly the sentiment. 'Men!' she breathed. It was an old joke, but Rob decided to humour Coll as he turned towards him grinning, 'No, Coll, I do not.'

Coll replied, 'They're feared it might lead to dancing . . .' and everyone laughed, Mary included.

It was a good night and it had only just begun. It was a long time since there had been any excuse for a celebration and the Gregorach were determined to make the most of it. Who could tell what the uncertain future held in store in these troubled times?

Sustained by the good meat and the aquavit the dancers reeled on, enlivened by the hard-driving pace of the fiddles. Rob watched them, thinking his own thoughts, as the curtains of dancers birled past him, faster and faster, arms linked to stop themselves flying apart.

He decided to rejoin the fray and threw himself at it with renewed energy. The hands were by now clapping and the feet stamping as Mary joined him. They knew that this frenzy of exertion could not last for ever, and the entire company was working itself up to one final climax of exuberance and oblivion, taking their lead from Rob and Mary.

It was well into the small hours of the morning when the company finally sank exhausted. The mood suddenly changed as the clear, unaccompanied sound of a solo voice took up one of the old Gaelic airs. The Gregorach had long been a dispossessed and hunted people, and the song told of their lost lands and the ancient wrongs that they had suffered. The listeners were transfixed by the heartbreaking melancholy and beauty of the words. As the singer drew to a close, many a hand rose to wipe a tear from the corner of an eye before the ensuing hush was followed by dignified but appreciative applause and then silence.

The first cold, grey flags of dawn were streaking the eastern skies over Glen Arklet when the pony made its way slowly up to the *clachan* and, home at last, lowered its head to graze. It was some time before anyone noticed it. When they did, a frightened cry went up, for they all recognized the mount. It was McDonald's.

Chapter Ten

This was not agreed

'A lesson that is quickly learned,
A signal this which all can see!
Thus nothing here provokes the strong
To wanton cruelty.'

On the morning appointed for McDonald's collection of the note of credit, Killearn had already been seated outside the tavern for some hours. Open in front of him on a table was a large battered ledger beside which his quill and sandbox lay. He was receiving, one by one, Montrose's tenants who had come to pay their quarter's rent. Most paid in coin, but some were paying with animals, grain and other payments in kind. They were deferential and apologetic when they had to offer goods in this way.

McDonald was patiently watching from the other side

of the track, sitting against a tree with the pony at his side. The day dragged as the line, never seeming to grow any smaller, slowly crept past. McDonald was becoming increasingly anxious and after an hour or so of this, eventually hauled himself up and went over to the table and addressed Killearn.

'Must I wait all day for my note, Killearn?'

Killearn barely looked up and said with some irritation, 'Patience, McGregor's man. Your turn is marked.'

Killearn went back to his collection and counting while McDonald, with a glare, went back to his position by the tree.

Several hours of this tense stand-off went by. McDonald had taken up a broadsheet on which there was news of a boat sailing to Virginia from Greenock, and he read the details avidly. From time to time he broke off to glance drowsily across at the table, where at last the queue was beginning to show some signs of coming to an end.

Yet more hours went by, and, try as he might, McDonald had been unable to stave off sleep. He lay in the sun, stretched out on the grass, with the broadsheet over his face. He was dimly aware of a shadow falling over him as the paper was snatched away, and McDonald woke with a start to find himself staring into the cold eyes of Killearn. Killearn calmly perused the document before finally addressing McGregor. 'Dreaming of the New World, were you?'

McDonald jerked himself upright, both muzzy-headed

and irritated. 'Dammit, Killearn, I have a long ride ahead of me and it grows dark. Have you the note?'

Killearn was quite unperturbed. 'My, but you're a zealot in McGregor's service. What loyalties the man commands – and him not even a chieftain.'

Killearn indicated the tavern with a nod of his head and turned towards it. McDonald could do nothing other than to follow him.

They entered the tavern and went into a small antechamber, where Killearn ordered a huddle of domino-players seated round a table to leave, with a peremptory jerk of the head. McDonald was unable to let this behaviour pass without comment. 'You are a Lowlander to the bone, Killearn. To your kind rank is all.'

Ignoring this, Killearn went behind the table and turned to address McDonald.

'I hear tell that in the New World they have your like – tribes of noble savages with paint on their faces and skins on their backs. You'll be well at home among them.'

McDonald, realizing that this was for the benefit of the listening ears in the main part of the tavern, shut the door and turned back towards Killearn.

'Enough of this. Have you the note?'

Killearn reached down under the table and brought up a small leather bag.

'His Lordship is to Edinburgh for the Assize. Then to London direct. Great doings at Court . . .'

McDonald stared at the bag as Killearn continued,

'And he's away without signing the note. The best I can do for you is coin.'

He placed the bag on the table so that McDonald could examine the contents.

'This was not agreed,' McDonald said quietly.

Killearn shrugged. 'Agreed or no, there's a thousand pound here. Count it or leave it, it makes no matter to me – or to His Grace.'

McDonald stared at him as Killearn met his eye and mused, 'It's a terrible shock to the system, the sight of a fortune within reach. Is it not?'

McDonald looked back at the money as Killearn continued, smiling: 'It's a great thing you have the trust of the McGregor, or I'd be hard pressed to sign it over.'

Killearn tipped the money out on the table and McDonald, after a momentary hesitation, sat down and doubtfully began to count it. He was so engrossed in his task – the money was a mixture of pound coin and smaller denominations – that he did not notice Killearn exchanging a few words with some of the occupants of the tavern before slipping off into the night.

While he steadily counted, McDonald's mind was in a turmoil as to what best to do next. It was by now pitch dark outside, and to travel with such an unheard-of sum of money was fraught with obvious dangers. On the other hand, he had been expected back hours before and Rob and the others would be waiting for him anxiously. Equally, who could tell what dangers might be lurking for him if he were to spend the night hard by the tavern, where he suspected others might have more than a good idea as to the contents of his bag?

It was not the kind of business that he had any stomach for – far better to be defending their herds in the lands of Balquhidder, broadsword in hand, side by side with the rest of the Gregorach. As he finished counting the money – it was exact to the nearest penny – he must have decided instinctively, for he knew not why himself, that his best course lay in taking to the road straight away.

Sweating the cold sweat of fear he saddled up his small wiry pony, wrapped his plaid around him tightly so as to conceal the bag of coin and the pistol which he laid across his saddle, and set off.

The first part of the journey was open and easy as he worked his way westwards along the lightly wooded fringes of Flanders Moss. Soon, however, the going became rougher and more treacherous as he left Buchlyvie behind him and gained height in the approach to the steadings at Drymen. It was now he realized that at some level, his thoughts had been telling him he had another choice, and he reined in his horse at a fork in the road.

To his right was the twisting and precipitous path along the side of Beinn Bhreac, and the way home. Ahead of him was the wider drove-road down to the crossing over the Clyde River at Dumbarton, and the way to Greenock and the New World. McDonald sat for a moment holding the pony still as it shifted uneasily beneath him, unable to understand this interruption in the accustomed route. He contemplated the choice, but then, with a shake of the head, turned his pony to the right and headed up the narrow path to the North.

He had hardly gone a dozen yards when he was startled by a sudden noise. It was the unmistakable sound of someone applauding. McDonald swung round to the source of the noise. Above him on the hillside under a large tree was a shortish man on horseback. It was Cunningham.

'Bravo, sir! A temptation faced is the Lord's delight,' he called out as he rode over and fell in slightly behind McDonald. McDonald did not stop but continued to ride, looking over his shoulder, his hand going instantly to the pistol under his plaid.

Cunningham continued to ride, now some twenty yards behind. McDonald desperately surveyed the trail ahead where it vanished under some trees in a dark tunnel. Cunningham shouted over, 'For a moment there I thought you might take the road to Greenock with your thousand pound.' And he laughed.

At this, McDonald swung round in the saddle and raised the pistol.

'Stay back! Or by God I'll shoot you dead.'

Cunningham smiled and kept on coming as, pulling out his sword, he quietly said, 'It's not so easy as it looks.'

McDonald pulled the trigger but the shot missed. Desperately he kicked his heels into the flanks of the pony and bolted for the trees, with Cunningham following at a full gallop.

If McDonald had hoped for an advantage by being the

first to gain the trees, it was but a small one. The branches tore at his face as he blundered desperately onward, the sound of hoofs never more than a few seconds behind. He quickly looked back and could see Cunningham gaining on him, riding like a madman whipping his mount with the flat of his sword. McDonald turned to face the way ahead again, concentrating hard in the darkness and redoubling his efforts. Suddenly he felt the wind being knocked clean out of him and he was brutally swept from the back of his mount which went galloping on.

A rope had been stretched between two trees across the path at exactly the height of a rider's neck. McDonald rolled helplessly on the trail as Cunningham, above him in an instant, summarily stabbed him in the chest without bothering to dismount.

But McDonald was not finished yet, and he managed to get to his feet before falling over again and then crashing off through the scrub and bracken. Cunningham quickly dismounted and was after him, almost casually stabbing at the injured man from time to time in the back, the neck, and the buttocks, much as a cat plays with an injured mouse. Eventually McDonald collapsed, facing down on a gentle slope, his head between the roots of a large tree, bleeding to death from his many wounds. Cunningham leaned over him and reached into the plaid for the bag he knew to be there. McDonald still clung to it, and Cunningham paused to study him as the dying man tried to crawl away down the slope.

Cunningham was in no hurry now. 'Thank your

Maker that you go before him without the sin of theft on your conscience – for a moment there it was a narrow margin.' He leaned over and stabbed McDonald again. This time it was final. Writhing and twisting on the ground, McDonald expired while Cunningham leaned down and gently relieved him of his treasure.

All that remained was to dispose of McDonald's body. This Cunningham easily achieved by dint of some well-selected stones to weigh it down, the proximity of the loch and a small rowing-boat. The remains of Alan McDonald hardly made a sound as they slipped over the stern and were sucked under the surface of the cold black waters.

Chapter Eleven

Not a bag of guineas

'All freakishness of mind is checked;
He tamed, who foolishly aspires;
While to the measures of his might
Each fashions his desires.'

Outside the tavern, a few of the Gregorach were standing in a group around McDonald's pony. They met the hostile stares of undisguised suspicion from the locals with a sullen silence.

Rob, who had come to find out what had happened, was inside the tavern with Alasdair and Coll by his side, standing face to face with Killearn. Killearn held the broadsheet which McDonald had been reading and was waving it in Rob's face. 'He sat out there all day pondering on this.'

Rob snatched it from Killearn's hand and contemptuously crumpling it up, threw it down behind him without looking at it.

'You gave him coin.'

Killearn sighed as if this was really the most tediously inconsequential business. 'When I told him His Grace had not signed the note he insisted on it – said you must have it or the beasts could not be bought at the best price.'

Alasdair bent over and picked up the broadsheet, and started to peruse it thoughtfully, his face becoming blacker and blacker.

Rob meanwhile was now in full flood. 'I am hard put to it to see you disgorge such a sum on the demand of one who would not bear the debt, Killearn.'

'He was your man, present at your signing of the terms. Ordered by you to wait . . .'

Rob roared in Killearn's face. 'For a note! Not a bag of guineas.'

Coll and Alasdair glanced at each other uneasily. They had never seen Rob lose control like this in the past. Killearn, too, was aware that he had Rob off balance and replied facetiously: 'It was not all guineas. These farmers pay in small coin, I assure you.'

Rob, refusing to be diverted by this, regained his control and asked quietly: 'He signed for this . . . this bag of coin?'

'Indeed he did.'

To prove the point, Killearn produced a piece of paper with a flourish and handed it over to Rob. Rob looked at it. It was McDonald's signature, sure enough. There was no doubt of that.

'Almost as bold a hand as yourself,' Killearn smirked.

Rob stared at him. Killearn's tone was grating on Rob's ever-growing anxiety.

'There had best be no malfeasance here, Killearn. This man stands under my protection.'

Killearn was enjoying the moment and made the most of it. 'Well, I am sure that is a great comfort to us all – what with a thousand pound at risk.'

Rob, furious at being baited in this way, swung round and strode out of the tavern, oblivious to the others. For his part, Killearn sat down, pleased with his performance and relaxed with all the satisfaction of a day's work well done. Nevertheless, it could have been a tense moment, and he was sufficiently relieved to call for a glass of aquavit.

Alasdair and Coll joined Rob and the rest of the Gregorach outside. Rob was standing silently, struggling to gain control of balanced measures of anger and worry. Equally silent, the others watched him anxiously. Eventually breaking the silence, Rob said quietly, 'We must search for Alan. I fear he is come to mischief hereabouts.'

Alasdair, who had been looking worried and sullen, burst out, 'I say we look for him in Greenock, Rob.' Alasdair held out the broadsheet, now uncrumpled to reveal the advertisement for the Greenock sailing. Rob stared at it for a moment and then at Alasdair.

'It comes quickly to your mind that he has robbed us, Alasdair.'

'He spoke of the Americas often enough . . .' Alasdair replied.

He looked around the others to solicit support, but, blank-faced, they merely stared at Rob.

Rob retorted disdainfully, 'And what, he walked to Greenock from Buchlyvie and sent his pony home without him . . .?'

Alasdair shrugged. He sensed Rob's anger but did not back down and continued, 'A thousand pound would buy him ten ponies and a trap to pull behind.'

'Alan McDonald did not betray me. Now to it and find his trace . . .' Rob looked around at the others and shouted, 'To it! To it!'

They all started to ready for the off. Only Rob and Alasdair were left standing. Alasdair looked at Rob, who stared back at him for a moment. Eventually Rob spat out: 'Go to Greenock then, since you have that stink in your nose. But Alasdair, bad enough that it might be so without you wish it.'

Alasdair thought on this for a moment, with a heavy heart that this should have come between him and Rob. Then, coming back to the here and now, he turned away and walked off, leaving Rob pensive.

It was the evening, and the Gregorach had had no success all day. There was no trace or word of McDonald anywhere. Dejected, they had given up for the night and taken shelter in a cave they knew well from better times.

Rob was standing at the entrance to the cave staring mournfully into the dark. It was a foul night and it was raining heavily, with cracks and flashes of thunder and lightning. Their horses were tethered outside while the men huddled round a fire inside, their shadows large upon the wall, trying to get warm as the damp steamed off their sodden clothing.

Rob was suddenly aware of a movement in the darkness, and discerned a figure approaching the cave. It was Alasdair, cold and soaking wet. Rob stared at him, interrogation spread across his face. Alasdair shook his head slowly. 'The ship sailed the day before I got there . . . His name was not on the harbour-master's list.'

Rob said nothing, but merely looked past Alasdair, and once again stared out into the night.

Alasdair too was silent for a moment, and then, unable to contain himself, blurted out: 'But he would not likely have given his own name and him run off with . . .' Rob's gaze made him trail off, and he went inside and dejectedly joined the others as Rob, silent, continued to stare into the storm.

CHAPTER TWELVE

You are the shite, Montrose

'All kinds and creatures, stand and fall,
By strength of prowess or of wit:
'Tis God's appointment who must sway,
And who is to submit.'

Montrose liked his club, and enjoyed the pleasantly decadent company he kept there It was a relief to get away from the rustic tedium of the country and pursue the game of intrigue and gossip – infinitely more exciting than the furred and feathered variety. Today he was relaxing over a hand of cards while the ever-present Cunningham watched over his shoulder.

So engrossed in the game was he that, when the doors at the end of the room suddenly and loudly slammed open, he remained completely unaware. It was the alert Cunningham who spotted the figure of an enraged Argyll burst into the room, look around, and then stride purposefully towards Montrose.

Cunningham whispered in Montrose's ear, 'Your Lordship, it is the Duke of Argyll come this way.'

Montrose, as befitted the atmosphere of the club, looked up languidly just as Argyll came to a halt at the table. Setting aside formality, Montrose addressed Argyll: 'John, you look like a man who means to play hard.'

Argyll's reaction was apoplectic. 'Do not presume to speak above your station, sir. I will have my rank from you.'

The voice thundered around the room and all the gaming tables fell silent. Montrose scarcely blinked, but he did deign to lay down his hand of cards.

'Your Grace.'

Argyll, unmollified, continued: 'I have word from Court that you are putting my name about as a Jacobite – as one who would rise for the Stewart should he land here to claim the throne.'

Impassively Montrose replied, 'Great men such as yourself draw rumours as shite draws flies.'

At this admittedly somewhat unflattering comparison, Argyll exploded. 'You are the shite, Montrose, and the flies upon it. I know you to the teeth. You are a man with twenty masks. I only marvel you do not have one that resembles a man. Keep your artificers off me. Off me! That is a warning.' Argyll half turned towards Cunningham. 'If you do not, this carrion-eater will not stand between us,' before storming out of the room.

Despite himself, even Montrose was shaken, although by anger rather than fear. He picked up his cards but was unable to set his mind to the game, and he threw them down, his face quivering.

'What pride, to use a fellow peer so – damn his pride. Pardon me . . . damn His Grace's pride.'

The other players were silent and merely stared at him open-mouthed, speculating as to what lay behind this exchange.

Chapter Thirteen

The only matter now

'Since, then, the rule of right is plain,
And longest life is but a day;
To have my ends, maintain my rights,
I'll take the shortest way.'

Inside Craigrostan House Rob was completely exhausted, and could only muster the strength to stare dejectedly into the fire. Mary was agitated and was berating him.

'Why is it so beyond your belief that he might have yielded to the sight of all that money put into his hands, unguarded, unasked, but there – a lifetime's wages in a bag?'

Rob stared up at her. 'Because I know him. I know him more than half his life.'

'Was he ever handed a thousand pound before?'

Rob was irritated. 'He was handed a hundred times more. He was given trust and he repaid in kind . . .'

Mary turned away, exasperated at this wilfulness, but Rob jumped up and pulled her round to face him.

'Why do you not believe me, woman?'

Mary, seeing his need to be right in his own eyes, conceded reluctantly. 'All right Rob, he did not steal from you. But he is gone and the money is gone and Montrose will not care if you believe one thing or the other.'

Rob slowly shook his head. 'That is another matter.'

Mary, exasperated, yelled at him: 'That is the only matter now!'

She seized his shoulders in order to be allowed to continue without interruption. 'For all our sakes, Robert, you must take off your high hat and make what terms you can, else Craigrostan is lost and ourselves His Lordship's tenants.'

The next morning a very different scene was being enacted outside Montrose's house. The great man, for so he regarded himself to be, resplendent in full regalia with wig and sword, was posing for a portrait. As ever, Cunningham, also bedecked rather splendidly, although he was not part of the painterly enterprise, was standing a few feet distant. Montrose surveyed his grounds in a proprietorial manner and espied Killearn leading Rob towards him. Rob was looking uncomfortable, bonnet in hand.

'Here comes our bold Highlander, no arse in his breeks and too proud to tug his forelock.'

Cunningham looked round languidly. 'No doubt the rogue will seek to blame his servant for the loss, for I hear there is no word of the man.'

Montrose gave him a shrewd look, and stepping out of his pose, said somewhat pointedly, 'I see you are back in favour with your tailor again, Archibald. He must be a happy man.'

Cunningham was rather uncertain what to read into this, but before he had time to concoct a response, Killearn was upon them with the Highlander in tow.

Rob made a short bow. 'My Lord.'

'So, McGregor, how is it with you?'

'As it was, my Lord. I have no word of McDonald or Your Lordship's money.'

Montrose looked at him closely. 'What are we to do, then?'

'If Your Lordship will contract with me for another sum, I will turn over all profit and so defray my debt.'

Montrose feigned amazement. 'I have but lost a thousand pound and you ask me to risk another?'

'My Lord, the money was stolen. From me and from you.'

'I am no part of your incompetence, McGregor. You have signed a paper.'

Rob replied stolidly, 'And I will honour it.'

Montrose began to show signs of irritation. 'Ply me not with your honour, man. Let us keep these matters simple. You are indebted to me. On that we are agreed.'

Rob held his ground, 'We are, my Lord.'

Montrose was silent for a moment, and seemed to stare distractedly into the middle distance. Then he turned back to look at Rob. 'Know you the Duke of Argyll?'

Rob was bewildered by this abrupt and inexplicable change of direction and wondered where it might be leading, but he nodded and said, 'By his repute alone.'

Montrose continued, 'My report is that Argyll is a Jacobite and would declare for James Stewart should he seek to reclaim the throne.'

Rob's face was expressionless. 'These are intelligences unknown to me, my Lord.'

Montrose faced him, and looked intently into the other man's eyes. 'They are known to you now.'

Rob was still searching in his mind for the shape to this, and shrewdly restricted himself to the noncommittal 'I am not certain of Your Lordship's meaning.'

Montrose suddenly became more forthright and revealed his hand. 'Dammit, man! You and your clan are Jacobites, are you not? Bred in the bone. Argyll is nothing to you. I want your word against him. Give it, and we will come to some reckoning on what you owe me.'

Rob was slightly dazed by this assault, but was acutely aware of the eyes of Cunningham and Killearn boring into him. At least he could begin to see what matters were afoot and he weighed them up for a moment before he replied, 'I can be of no assistance to Your Lordship in this matter of the Duke of Argyll.'

Montrose stiffened and hissed, 'You owe me, McGregor.'

Rob replied quietly, as if pointing out the obvious, 'I owe you money. Nothing more. What you have asked is as below me as it should be beneath Your Lordship.'

Montrose was seething with malice. 'You misspeak yourself, McGregor.'

Rob was unmoved. 'It is the Marquis of Montrose who has misspoken himself to ask my perjury against his enemies.'

Montrose stiffened visibly at these words while Cunningham grabbed Rob, pulled him round by the shoulder and broke in: 'You were better dead after this insult.'

Cunningham's hand was already on the handle of his sword. Rob was aware of this, but didn't allow his eyes to stray from Montrose's face for a moment.

'Leave the blade be, sir. This is not your quarrel.'

Montrose interjected across this. 'You do not seem to hear me, McGregor. I did not ask you if or whether. Your land is forfeit to me against your debt. Until that is settled, I will have you lodged in the Tolbooth – take him into custody, Archibald. You have my commission on it.'

Cunningham's face seemed to brighten at these words, for he caught a whiff of advancement for himself in this whole affair. His hand went readily to his sword again, but before it was clear of its scabbard Rob had magicked a small dirk out of the folds of his bonnet. With a flash it was under Cunningham's chin, forcing his head up and back. All of this had somehow happened without Rob's eyes ever having left Montrose's face, which he now addressed.

'My father lay two years in the Booth for no cause but the will of great men, and I will not go there, sir.'

At this, Rob raised the dirk higher with a jerk and blood was now dripping down the blade from where it had punctured the skin. Still Rob's eyes never shifted from Montrose's face as he looked past that of the stricken Cunningham. Montrose stared at Killearn, 'Call out the watch, damn you . . .'

'Call nothing or I will cut his throat,' Rob interrupted.

Montrose was almost unbelieving at this unpredicted turn of events. 'You are damned, McGregor, damned to hell.'

As he started to frogmarch Cunningham away, Rob almost quipped, 'Come, Your Lordship, leave the devil some work. You have done enough for one day.'

Rob reached down, and pulling out Cunningham's sword, sent it whirling in a huge arc far across the gardens. Then, pausing only to dispatch Cunningham staggering backward into a formal bed of flowers with a violent thrust of his leg, he was off, running like a deer to where his pony was waiting. All the time Montrose, who seemed to be on the verge of some kind of seizure, was screaming at the paralysed Killearn: 'Call out the watch, call out the watch!'

Finally Killearn managed to regain control of his limbs, and ran lumberingly towards the house as Cunningham struggled to his feet and dusted himself down. Montrose stared after Rob, who was now riding away from the grounds, and muttered with a vitriolic malice, 'You have slept your last peaceful night, McGregor. You and yours.'

CHAPTER FOURTEEN

The house of fear

So was it – would, *at least have been*
But through untowardness of fate;
For polity was then too strong –
He came an age too late;

Rob was back at Craigrostan House and was hurriedly packing a bag with provisions, while Mary stood over him and watched. Outside a few of the Gregorach were milling around talking in low voices, exchanging the word on events. Mary was trying to question Rob, but his thoughts seemed far away.

'What is John Campbell, Duke of Argyll, to us, Robert, that you must defend him against Montrose?'

Rob brushed past her as he headed towards the door, saying, in an exasperated tone – as if this made everything clear – 'I did not defend him. I refused to bear false witness against him.'

Mary stared after him as Rob addressed Gregor. 'Send men to the passes and set watches.'

Gregor nodded and asked, 'And the lochside?'

Rob thought for a moment. 'They'll not likely come along the shore, but watch all ways . . .' He turned round and caught sight of Duncan and Ranald, who were agog with excitement at the sight of Rob's naked sword lying on the table. He looked them straight in the eye. 'Now listen, lads, I must go to the hills for a time. You stay by your mother and be her help.'

Mary broke in at this. 'At least let Argyll know you are persecuted for his sake.'

'I am persecuted, Mary, for no man's sake but my own.'

This avowal was made in a tone which was neither self-righteous nor pompous but something far, far deeper and heartfelt. It was the voice of a man shouting across the abyss of gender to the uncomprehending ear of a woman. He was not so far gone as to be unable to see this in her face as she turned away. He went over to her and asked, almost supplicating, 'What, would you have me lie against all conscience to suit Montrose?'

Mary was stung by her failure to make him understand and she turned on him angrily: 'No, to suit me and Duncan and Ranald!' As this obviously got through to him she could not resist hammering home the rest. 'To stay home with your wife and children instead of taking to the hills like a fox.'

More of the Gregorach appeared at the door, Alasdair among them. To a man they were all armed. Rob looked over at them standing together, framed in the doorway, and then he looked back at Mary. Mary had wanted this to be private, and, although she would never have admitted it, was more than a little jealous of the bonds of unshakeable male loyalty which tied the Gregorach to her husband. She shouted, 'Out, out! He'll be with you soon enough.'

The men backed away uncomfortably at this as Rob, feeling wrong-footed at every turn, tried to comfort Mary.

'Mary, take the lads and away to Morag's. They'll make a place—'

But Mary cut him off abruptly. 'And let Montrose's troopers foul my house?'

'No injury will come to you. Montrose's quarrel is with me.'

They were totally at odds now, and Mary continued spitefully: 'And you revel in it. The great man against all . . . And likely you'll slip down in the night when the mood takes you, or will you just find yourself a sheep to comfort you . . . ?'

Rob was both shocked and angry at the same time. Mary saw that she had hit home as Rob looked over at the boys, who seemed not to have noticed any of this, since they were too preoccupied in watching the assembled Gregorach outside. Rob's face tightened as he seized up his bag.

'Aye, well if I do, it'll be one that doesn't bleat so bitter.'

And he was gone, while Mary, angry at herself and at him, closed her eyes and tried to resume some sense of control.

Rob and Coll headed up urgently from behind Craigrostan House to the ridge above. Rob was issuing his instructions.

'Now, no trouble between them and you. Give no cause. This is between me and Montrose, and likely when he's broken a few horses, he'll quieten down. Watch Alasdair, put him where he can do no harm . . .' He stopped and turned to Coll. 'And Coll, keep up the watch for McDonald.'

Coll made a wry face. 'Ach Rob, he's long gone.'

'Aye, but is he over the seas or under them?' Rob, as if putting this thought behind him, paused before continuing, his voice concerned: 'And ask Morag to go down to Mary. She is bitter with me for this business.'

Rob reflected for a moment before changing the subject entirely. 'That Montrose is a stoat of a man. Heaven protect us from his like.'

Coll's eyes lit up as he pronounced with a touchingly naïve faith, 'When the King comes across the water again, we'll see him hanged.'

But Rob shook his head with what seemed a deep melancholy. It was clear that, much as he might like to, he put little store by such an outcome. Rather than say anything, they embraced and Rob was away, driving himself on, ever upwards towards the distant ridge.

Coll came back down and was joined by Alasdair at a rocky outcrop over the loch. The impetuous Alasdair was vehement in his protestations.

'Instead of spying them out we should lie for them, cut them down in the passes.'

Coll was rather more phlegmatic about this opinion. 'Aye, a wee war with Montrose would suit us fine.' He paused, remembering Rob's warning, and then admonished: 'Keep your watch, give warning and stay your hand, Alasdair Roy, or you'll have to answer to me.'

Alasdair threw down his kit in disgust and stared out across the loch. 'Damn, that McDonald has brought this on us. I never trusted the man – always at Rob's arse like a collie dog.'

Coll gave a kind of shrug and mused, 'Morag had a dream on him. Saw him drowned.'

Alasdair picked up a rock and hurled it out over the loch with savage satisfaction. 'Aye, maybe his ship sank and him loaded down with his theft.'

Out on the waters of the loch the stone splashed, silently sending out slow ripples.

In the courtyard of Montrose's house, Cunningham, dressed resplendently in his rather too stylish notion of what passed for military dress, was astride his horse and looking up at Montrose, who stood on a balcony where the portrait-painting exercise was in progress once again. A troop of horsemen were waiting in the yard, the somewhat unmilitary figure of Killearn amongst them.

Cunningham shouted up, rather uncertainly it seemed, despite his confident words; 'Your Lordship will not regret leaving this matter in my hands. I have some knowledge of how best to bring rogues like these to heel.'

Montrose replied enigmatically: 'Broken but not dead, Archibald. That is all I ask.'

Cunningham raised his glass. 'No commander could ask for more latitude – "Broken but not dead!" – It has a ring to it.'

Montrose was under no illusions. 'I think you may find him an elusive rogue; by all reports he knows his hills like a flea knows its dog.'

'Then we must scratch where he cannot hide.' And Cunningham drank, well pleased with his new-found purpose in life.

Montrose watched for a moment, then turned back to the matter in hand – the portrait – as the horsemen rode out noisily from the courtyard below, watched by the assembled servants, Betty among them.

That night Rob was laid up in the heather high above the loch, wrapped in his plaid, eyes on the clear night sky which was encrusted with stars. His thoughts were on Mary.

At the same moment, Mary was standing outside Craigrostan House. Her eyes were also fixed on the heavens. After a long moment she shook her head, turned and went inside. The dog took up its usual nightly position and lay down across the threshold. Mary touched its head as she went past.

In the woods on the lower slopes above the loch, Cunningham and Killearn were huddled next to a listless fire. The horses were tethered near by but the troopers were some distance away. Trying to put some life into the fire, Cunningham prodded a log with the toe of his boot, his face thoughtful. As if this action needed some response, Killearn mused, 'He'll not be sitting home waiting for us, and he can hide in these hills till we're wore out.'

Cunningham seemed quite unperturbed. 'We'll bring him to us. Have no fear.'

Killearn kept the ball rolling. 'Oh, and how will we do that, Archie?'

'If this rogue has the high opinion of himself that he has displayed before His Lordship, there are matters he will not abide. Believe me, I know what raises a man's blood to the boil . . . With brutes, the way is brutality – liberally applied.'

Killearn stared at Cunningham, puzzling as to his meaning. Cunningham shot him a significant look before returning his inscrutable gaze to the heart of the fire.

Chapter Fifteen

You do not ask a whore

Or shall we say an age too soon?
For, were the bold man living now,
How might he flourish in his pride,
With buds on every bough!

At Craigrostan House Mary awoke early. She lay still for a moment while she realized that she was once again on her own, and then tried to make sense of the events of the previous day. Eventually, she hauled herself out of the bed. As usual, she checked the fire and put a slab of peat on the grey embers, picked up a shawl and opened the door to be greeted by the damp dog.

Mary walked down over the soft turf and gently sloping soft grey shingle to the lochside. The loch was still shrouded in mist, and this blocked out all sound. At the water's edge, the dog beside her, she squatted down to urinate, being careful to keep her shift and shawl out of the chill waters of the loch, and stared out into the mist.

She rose, shivering slightly, and rearranged her shawl around her. Suddenly, the dog at her side started to growl. Puzzled, Mary looked at the dog and then around behind her, to see what was concerning the animal. There was nothing to be seen, yet it continued to growl as she tried to hush it. Then she saw, forming itself in the mist, the shape of a longboat, its banks of oars slowly beating, a man standing upright in the prow. It was clearly headed straight for the precise part of the shore where she was standing.

She stared transfixed by what seemed, for a moment, to be an apparition. Then as the dog began to bark hysterically, she suddenly realized what was happening and turned round to run back to the house, screaming the boys' names. The dog stayed at the water's edge, frantically running from side to side and barking as the longboat closed on the spot.

In the prow, Cunningham picked up a musket and, bracing himself as the boat began to grate against the shingle, took aim at the dog and gently – ever so gently – squeezed the trigger. The dog was knocked into the air and back half a dozen yards by the impact of the ball. Cunningham replaced the weapon in the bilges and smiled a quiet smile of satisfaction at his prowess.

Mary had just reached the house when the sound of

the shot achieved what her cries had failed to do and wakened the sleeping boys.

She screamed at them, 'Run, boys, run to Coll's house, raise them . . . they have come by the loch!'

The sound of the shot travelled across the loch and, ever fainter and fainter, echoed off the steep hillsides on either shore. It finally reached Alasdair, who was keeping watch hunched up against a rock on the hillside high above Craigrostan. It disturbed his sleep for a moment, but not enough to wake him, and after a brief start, his head dropped down again into slumber.

The boat was well up on the shingle and the oars were being shipped as Cunningham leapt lightly over the prow, and the troopers clambered over the sides to pull it further up the beach.

At the house, Mary had the boys up and, still dazed, scrambling into their clothes. Ranald saw the body of the dead dog. Instantly, he cried out and started towards it and the advancing troopers, as Mary pulled him back.

'Leave him. Go, go, bring the Gregorach.'

At this, the boys started away up the track behind the house. Watching them go, Mary turned and pulled her shawl around her before going back to stand defiantly in front of her home.

She could see Cunningham leading the little group of men up the slope to the house. She contemplated them without any fear now – only anger and a kind of contempt. Cunningham attained the front door of the house and came to a halt, 'I have come for the outlaw, Robert McGregor.'

'If you think he would be lying in his bed waiting for you, then you are more of a fool than you look.'

Without hesitating, Cunningham hit her hard in the pit of the stomach, winding her and doubling her up. As she staggered back into the doorway, he turned to the troopers, 'Search the outsheds and burn them . . . kill the stock.'

Killearn came out from amongst the other men and stared at Mary who was righting herself, still defiant, and addressed her. 'You had best stand aside, Mistress McGregor.'

Cunningham looked sideways at him contemptuously. 'You do not ask a whore, you make her.' As if to demonstrate, he walked up, caught Mary by the hair and dragged her inside. Killearn went over to the door and started to watch. His eyes bulging with shock, he stared with a kind of horrified excitement at the scene unfolding in front of him.

Cunningham had ripped back Mary's skirt and shift and forced her, face down, forward over the table and began to undo his breeches. Killearn realized what was going to happen and called out, 'Archie,' more in disbelief than in protest. Then, seeing the inevitable, he stepped inside, closed the door behind him and stayed within to witness the brutal conclusion.

Behind the house the troopers were setting fire to the thatch of the outlying sheds and shooting and stabbing the livestock as the beasts stood at their stalls in the byres.

The shots echoed off the hillsides and this time the sound was sufficient to penetrate Alasdair's slumbers and rouse him. He listened for a moment and then, realizing the import of the noise, leapt up, seized his sword and started to run down the hill.

Cunningham was standing between Mary's knees, holding her body pinned face down on the table, with one hand on the scruff of her neck, the other pressing her buttocks down. He was in her up to the hilt, and pushing with long, heavy repeated thrusts. Killearn stood by the door, totally transfixed by the scene, both alarm and a sort of glazed excitement in his eyes.

Cunningham finished off, enjoying a long satisfied spasm at the end. He turned round and looked at Killearn.

'Do you want your share, Killearn, now that I've loosened her up for you?'

Killearn was aghast and fearful at hearing his name spoken out loud, and urgently shaking his head began to back out of the house.

As Cunningham stepped back and adjusted his dress, Mary lay still for a moment. Then she drew herself up and dragged her shawl over her nakedness. She stared back at Cunningham who was watching her. He completed his readjustments.

'Think of yourself as the scabbard and me the sword, Mistress McGregor – and a fine fit you were.'

Refusing to be cowed, she held her stare. 'I will think of you as dead until my husband makes you so, and then I will think on you no more.'

Cunningham nodded curtly as he headed for the door and opened it.

'Indeed, such a man as he will need to see blood on his blade before honour is satisfied . . . Tell him Archibald Cunningham is at his service.'

He stepped out into the morning light and closed the door behind him, leaving her inside, the full horror of the event beginning to engulf her. She began to shudder, but with a huge effort she regained control, and a little unsteadily, eased herself down off the table.

By now the outbuildings were all ablaze and the livestock dead. Well satisfied, the troopers began to drift back from their predations. Cunningham joined Killearn, who regarded him with new eyes. As the troopers came up to the house, Cunningham ordered one of them to put a torch to it. The trooper looked uncertain and asked if the woman was still inside.

His reply was coldly pragmatic. 'Set a light and we'll see her out . . .' Killearn looked at Cunningham as the trooper flung the blazing brand up into the thatch. Cunningham met his gaze. 'What are you gawking at? Have you never been to war before?'

Killearn replied with a shaky admiration, 'Oh, you are a warrior, Archie, and no mistake . . .'

The fire caught and the thatch began to burn, flinging

high into the sky black and red streamers of smoke and flame which the now frantic Alasdair could see as he ran down the hillside above.

Mary was still inside in an emotionless trance, combing her hair – her face like stone. The thatch was fully ablaze by now and as time passed and Mary still did not emerge, Killearn was becoming more and more agitated.

'If she does not come out there will be a reckoning, Archie. Shagging her's one thing, burning her's another.'

Cunningham's reply was laconic; 'She'll come out. That one is a hater.'

As he spoke the door was opened gently and Mary stepped out. She seemed perfectly calm as she walked through the small crowd of troopers, past Cunningham and Killearn without even glancing at them, and onward down to the lochside. The troopers stared at her, beginning to wonder if something more than they knew had taken place. Cunningham saw this, and quickly ordered them back to the boat. They fell back from the house which was now ablaze inside as well as out, and made their way down to the boat followed by Cunningham and Killearn.

They came up behind Mary who stopped, gazing straight ahead, to let them get past. As he drew level with her, Killearn could not resist making his own venal contribution to the atrocity, and whispered in her ear: 'They say it's not a sin if you don't take pleasure in it.'

He instantly regretted this, for she turned and looked at him straight in the face with a stare that scorched him to the quick. In a panic he stumbled after Cunningham, and followed him down to the boat which was already being pushed out by the troopers.

Mary waited until it was well afloat, then walked on down to the water, past the body of the dead dog, and wading in up to her thighs, began to scrub herself between the legs.

Behind her, Alasdair cleared the woods. In an instant he took in the blazing house and the retreating boat. With a yell of impotent rage he ran down to the shore, ignoring Mary in the heat of the moment.

Chapter Sixteen

Oh, pay he will . . . There is honour here

Then rents and factors, rights of chase,
Sheriffs, and lairds and their domains,
Would all have seemed but paltry things,
Not worth a moment's pains.

In a narrow gully, on the slopes of Cruinn a' Bheinn to the east of Craigrostan, Rob was checking the trap he had set. There was a rabbit in it but a fox had got there first and the rabbit was half-eaten. He shook his head with a little smile as if reflecting upon the ways of the wilderness.

Above him a lark was singing, rising and dropping in the brightening light. Rob picked up what remained of the rabbit and paused to watch the bird. It drew his eyes to the ridge at the edge of the gully and it was then that he saw the thin plume of smoke rising in the clear air. He started, and then stared at it for a moment as one thought formed in his mind – Mary – and he began to run.

At Craigrostan House Alasdair ran out into the water but the longboat was already well under way, leaving a spreading herring-bone of a wake behind it and banking its oars powerfully. He was waist deep and screaming, thrashing the water with his broadsword in a by now futile frenzy.

Cunningham, complacently thinking to repeat his recent feat of marksmanship, raised his musket, took aim at the figure in the loch and fired. But the rocking of the boat disturbed the shot and the ball ploughed the surface of the water harmlessly.

Killearn grinned. 'You're a better aim with dogs and quim, Archie.' Then he leaned out over the side of the boat and made his 'baa-ing' noise before settling back with a great feeling of satisfaction.

In the water, Alasdair was close to tears at his helplessness. The troopers in the boat now took up Killearn's lead, and the derisive sound came wafting back over the waters of the loch like an obscene smell. Despairing, Alasdair turned away, and it was only then that he really saw Mary. Concerned and not a little puzzled, he waded over to find out what she was doing.

Mary was totally self-absorbed. All her anger and shock was focused between her thighs as she splashed and scraped. She didn't look up until Alasdair, from only a few feet away, asked, 'Mary, are you hurt? Did they wound you?'

She looked up with a terrible unfocused, empty gaze. In a flash the callow boy suddenly grew up as he realized what had happened and he sank to his knees in the water as if felled by a powerful blow.

'... Oh Mary, Mary. What have they done ...?'

She stood and looked vacantly at the blazing house for a moment. Then, with an enormous effort of will, she gathered herself together as Alasdair went gibbering on.

'... We will avenge you ... Rob will kill them, every last one of them.'

After what seemed like an eternity, she turned at last to Alasdair and looked at him. When she eventually did speak it was in a low, intense voice, scarcely recognizable as her own.

'He will not know. Rob will not know.'

Alasdair was stunned and perplexed. 'But Mary, he must know.'

'He will not, you hear me, Alasdair McGregor. I will not tell him and you will not,' she screamed at him.

She went over to him and forcibly jerked him to his feet. Alasdair shook his head in incomprehension.

'But Mary ...'

Mary saw in his eyes that he didn't understand, and started to shake him violently.

'It is what they want. What the Englishman wants. It is his plan ... You will swear it, your silence, swear it!'

'I cannot.'

'You can. If I can bear it to be done, you can bear to be silent . . . swear it!'

Alasdair was dumbstruck by her fierceness and nodded, but she kept hold of him with both hands and shook him until she was sure that he was fully conscious of his pledge.

Behind them the house, with a great gust of flame, finally collapsed. Only then did Mary release Alasdair, pushing him away and saying in a low flat voice, 'And I will hold you to it, mark me.'

That night, the whole community was gathered at the *clachan* near Craigrostan pressing in on Rob, Mary and Alasdair, who still bore a stricken look. One after another the men spoke, Coll first.

'Send to Speyside with the signal, Rob, raise the clan.'

Gregor was in agreement. 'Call out Iain Glas and Duncan Og; we can have two hundred afore another nightfall.'

'It is beyond bearing that they should show such offence to a defenceless woman,' Iain added.

Alasdair twitched and jerked as he caught Coll's eye and said, as if there were hidden significance to his words, 'Let us go among them, Rob, for what they have done to Mary . . .'

At this Mary shot him a glance which made the words dry up on his tongue while Rob, too preoccupied to notice any of this, finally spoke.

'It's a sore thing they have laid on us, on Mary, on me.

Far past any wrong I had expected, even from such as Montrose.'

Gregor filled the silence. 'He must pay, Rob – else what are we?'

Rob nodded grimly, his anger bottled within. 'Oh, pay he will, till his teeth squeal. But think on it now, think on it. Even if we raised the McGregors of Speyside and the McGregors of Lochee, if we called upon our kin to gather, we cannot, could not, must not, fight Montrose in open battle. He has ten times – twenty times – our numbers and the strength of the Crown to back him . . .'

There was a murmur of protest at this, for it went against all notions of honour and natural justice. Rob let this subside but Gregor added, to great and general applause, 'There is honour here. You are wronged, Mary is wronged – and us with you.'

Rob waited until the applause had died down before replying: 'Honour will be satisfied, you know me well enough. But consider what we are owed. Cattle killed, a house burned, but none are dead, none injured . . .'

At this, Alasdair choked and stared at Mary who returned his gaze, blank-eyed, as Rob continued. 'We will cost Montrose dear, I promise. But listen, we cling to our living by nail and teeth as it is. Give that man warrant to raise fire and sword and we'll sleep in the hills this winter and bury our weans in the spring.'

The reality of what he was saying began to get through to them, and the pragmatic Coll began to nod heavily. 'Rob is right. It is not within our reach to harm such as Montrose.'

But now Rob's rage finally burst forth with an awesome hissing certainty, 'Oh we'll harm him all right, never fear, but this matter began with money and will end with money. The tenderest part of James Graham is his purse, and we'll hurt him sure in it . . . cattle and rent, rent and cattle, till his coffers are bled.'

And a growl of agreement went round as, not for the first time, he carried the men of the Gregorach with him. Mary sat still, staring before her. When the noise abated, Morag looked over at her and said into the quiet, 'We have not heard Mary on it, and in truth she it was who was the most affronted.'

All eyes turned to Mary in concern and sympathy. Rob suddenly cast aside his own thoughts and his hand reached for her shoulder. She looked up at him, and then far away into the darkness. Alasdair stared at her, terrified she would speak, fearful that she would not. After a long moment she stood up and responded with a deep-rooted Scottish stoicism.

'Rob is right. What can't be helped must be endured.'

At this she turned and made her way through the small but tightly packed throng, which was strangely puzzled and hushed at her sudden exit.

Later that night Rob, Mary and the boys were taking refuge in Coll's cottage. The boys were asleep and Mary was also in bed, her face to the wall but wide awake, while Rob sat beside her, sore troubled. He looked at the silent shape of her back but knew she was not asleep.

'I should have been with you, Mary. It was not fit I was in the hills.'

'Then you would be dead now.' She did not turn round.

Rob stared at her and shook his head. 'No, they would have took me to the Tolbooth.'

Mary stared at the bleak wall. 'No, I think you would be dead.'

Rob reached out to her shoulder, and pulling himself on to the bed lay down beside her, but his hand encountered nothing but her silent bulk, obdurate as stone.

Outside, Alasdair sat with Coll and Gregor around a small fire. Alasdair was agitated and repeatedly plunged his dirk into the turf between his feet.

'They "baa-ed" at me. I cursed them and called them to fight.' He stared up at the others wildly, 'I could do nothing.'

Coll was sympathetic and conciliatory. 'No man says you could, Alasdair Roy.'

Alasdair was not in any mood to be placated. 'I will kill me one, I swear it. Cattle and rent will not suffice, for all Rob says. There's more needed, there's blood called for here.'

The other two looked at him doubtfully and wondered if this was just the usual Alasdair letting his words overreach themselves as ever – or was there something more to it than that?

Chapter Seventeen

The conspirator's mind

Rob Roy had never lingered here,
To these few meagre Vales confined;
But thought how wide the world, the times
How fairly to his mind!

Inside a chamber at Montrose's house, Montrose and Cunningham were holding what passed for a council of war. Killearn was also present but not as a main protagonist. Montrose was staring at the wall, deep in thought, and then he turned back to Cunningham for confirmation. 'But of McGregor himself, no word . . . is that so?' His voice was sharp and dissatisfied.

'We will have him soon enough. I have set such an affront to his Highland honour that he will come to redeem it, mark me.'

Montrose looked at him quizzically for a moment

before deciding to let this comment pass, and turned instead to Killearn, perhaps feeling that here was a more profitable line of inquiry. 'How say you to this?'

Killearn beamed. 'Indeed, Mr Cunningham did leave such a mark that McGregor will come to rub it out, or else he is not the man he takes himself to be.'

Montrose sensed there was more to this enigma than he needed or wanted to know, and looked at them both squarely, 'Very well . . . but see to it that I am not mocked. In the meantime, make my claim against these acres on Lomondside for the debt he owes.'

Then he reflected for a moment. '. . .Still no word of this man of McGregor's, he who took the coin?'

Killearn replied, 'Not a word, my Lord.'

Cunningham rather too hastily chipped in, 'Nor will there be. This was a ploy of McGregor's – to take the money and blame another. His man is well hid and Your Lordship's money well spent, I wager it.'

Montrose's eyes flickered over Cunningham in that way which always unsettled the Englishman, for he never knew what to read into that look. 'My, my, you have a rare grasp of the conspirator's mind, Archibald. You are to be commended on it.'

On balance, Cunningham decided to appear to take this as a compliment and he made a short bow.

Later, as Cunningham and Killearn were walking back to Cunningham's quarters in the coach-house, Killearn was nervously trying to make the other man appraise the subtleties of the situation.

'He sees through it, Archie, I know him and his gibes.'

Cunningham was quickly defensive. He did not like any suggestion that he was not the intellectual master of events. 'And you think he would count it against us if he knew? He has his three hundred acres for only a thousand pound. A fair price by any reckoning.' And he attempted to give the impression that this manner of reasoning had been uppermost in his mind all along.

Killearn was far from convinced.

As they approached the entrance to the coach-house, a figure stepped forward from the shadows. It was a very distraught Betty who seemed to have been waiting there for some time. She burst out: 'Archie, sir . . . I must speak with you . . .' and then she recognized Killearn and shrank away from him, but eventually composed herself and decided to continue nevertheless; 'I am dismissed from service on account of my state.'

Cunningham was unperturbed. 'And what is your state, pretty Betty?'

'You know well, I am with your child . . . and he – this one – has made report of it.'

Killearn scoffed, 'Ach, Betty, my report did nothing your belly would not have announced on its own.'

Betty, distraught, seized Cunningham. 'Archie, I love you. What am I to do?'

'Root the bastard out. If Killearn here does not know a crone with a twig, I miss my guess.'

Betty shook her head. 'It's too far gone for that.'

Cunningham sneered with some heat, 'Then it will not be the first bastard born in Scotland.'

The woman screamed at him, hysterically beating on

his chest and at his head. He made no attempt to defend himself but waited until she stopped, exhausted, sobbing and shaken. Cunningham looked at her for a moment before walking on. Killearn, ever eager for insight into the mysteries of evil, hurried after him and caught up.

'My, Archie, you are a villain to envy. How do you achieve such ease in the part?'

Cunningham walked on without looking back. His face was set with the kind of pain that is the mirror image of the pleasures of cruelty. Eventually he replied languidly, 'I rehearse. How else?'

Delighted with this gem, Killearn shook his head in awe and added, somewhat enigmatically, 'One must give God his due. He is an indifferent playwright, but he picks his players to perfection.'

They walked on as Betty, shaking with her helplessness, receded into the darkness behind them.

CHAPTER EIGHTEEN

The truth is but a lie undiscovered

And to his Sword he would have said,
'Do Thou my sovereign will enact
From land to land through half the earth!
Judge thou of law and fact!

The small cart creaked and groaned along the rutted track on the southern fringes of Rannoch Moor. Mary was in the cart with a few items of domestic necessity. Alongside walked Rob with the two boys. As they approached the house it was plain that it had not been occupied for some time. Rob could see Mary's expression as she surveyed the nettles against the wall, the thistles in the thatch . . .

'It'll look more like itself when the sun shines,' he ventured hopefully.

Silent, Mary got down and went into the house and

looked around the dank interior. Rob came in behind her, put his hand on her shoulder and inclined his head towards hers.

'. . .When we have our bed in it and us in our bed, it will seem home enough.'

Her face remained unmoved at such a prospect, and she turned back to the boys who were already starting to explore.

'All right. We have work to do. Play can wait . . .'

Her manner left Rob standing in the doorway, feeling bereft.

A band of the Gregorach, mostly on foot but with a few mounted men, were driving a herd of cattle through the strath of a long glen. Rob came riding up to a group where Alasdair had his dagger at the throat of a man whose son, a boy scarcely older than Rob's own, watched in terror.

Rob spoke. 'What's amiss here?'

Alasdair replied, 'One of Montrose's men, trying to claim these beasts are his and not his master's.'

The stockman spoke up. 'I am not Montrose's man. He feeds his cattle on my pasture and mine are among his. You have my beasts as well as Montrose's.'

Rob looked at him. The man was clearly frightened but determined to make his point. Rob turned to look at the boy.

'Is this true, lad?'

'Aye . . . aye.'

Rob continued to address his questions to the boy. 'Do you know your beasts?'

'Aye, two brindles and a Galloway – the Galloway is mine.'

Rob nodded, then turned back to the man. 'That's a good lad you have there. Cut out your cattle . . . Put up, Alasdair,' and Alasdair reluctantly lowered his dagger while the man and boy went off to recover their own cattle.

Alasdair was unrepentant. 'He pays rent to Montrose. If you would hurt His Lordship, you needs must hurt his tenants.'

Rob ignored this, impatient. 'Drive cattle, man. We haven't all day.'

Rob rode off leaving Alasdair, angry at this dismissal, to get on with the herding.

Outside the house on Rannoch Moor there were already signs of improvement. The weeds and nettles had been cleared and the gaps in the walls filled in. Smoke rose from the chimney, and the boys were playing happily on the hillside behind in the golden evening light. It was all in all a perfect domestic scene.

Inside, however, things were not so carefree. Betty Sturrock was sitting at the table. She was now noticeably pregnant. Mary was sitting opposite her, listening to her tale, her face grave and full of sympathetic concern. Betty continued to spill it out, breathlessly and confidentially, woman to woman. 'I could not hear all of it, but Killearn talked of money, that Archie might take . . .'

Mary clarified: 'This is Cunningham? This "Archie"?'
Betty nodded. 'He is wild, but it is that Killearn. He has the devil in him.'

Mary, feeling no reason to debate this, pressed on: 'Tell me about this money, did you hear a sum spoken?'

'Archie said it would be the easiest thousand pound he ever earned. The only pity that it would be in Scots and not English pounds.'

'And how did he mean to earn this thousand pound?'

'I know not, save that Killearn said no trace must be left . . .'

Mary absorbed this and then looked back at Betty with some purpose. 'My husband will appreciate that you came with this word. Will you take some supper and rest, Betty, for you look ill-used?'

'Oh, I am not worse used than I deserve, Mistress McGregor, for I have a bastard's bastard in me and no home for him when he comes out.'

Mary shrugged this off and went over to the press, tight-lipped, and took out some bread. 'Well, we'd better feed you or he'll not have the strength to try.' Hearing Betty sobbing behind her, she turned and went back to put an arm around the distraught child, for, in truth, she was little more than such. 'Lass, lass, bear up now. Your bairn will have you and you will have it.'

The following morning Rob and Mary were pondering the import of Betty's words. Rob was pacing back and forth, not quite knowing what to make of it and swinging from one violent reaction to another. 'I know it, I know they plotted against us. Damn them that they carried it through . . .' He turned and paused, attempting to gather his resolve amidst the fury of his reactions: 'We will have them before the Assize, Killearn and Cunningham, aye and Montrose too, if he were part of it.'

Mary was less sanguine; 'Do you think such men as these will admit this because wee Betty Sturrock, with her belly under her chin, says so?'

Rob turned, puzzled. 'What's her belly to do with it?'

Mary explained, exasperated: 'She is carrying the Englishman's child. They will call her a whore came for revenge.'

Rob thought on this for a moment, but continued, somewhat unconvinced. 'They may say what they like. She will speak the truth.'

'Robert, to these men the truth is but a lie undiscovered.'

He turned back to her forcibly, tears rising in his eyes, 'I will have justice! . . . Alan McDonald is dead, woman.'

Mary pressed her more pragmatic line. 'Then take your case to the Duke of Argyll. You are in this matter on account of him; it is known he bears Montrose no favour.'

But this didn't sit well with Rob's sense of honour and his voice was almost scornful; 'You put great store by wolves of different shades. They are all alike at lambing.'

Mary was despairing of the man. 'And you will have nothing but your own way! I tell you, Killearn and

Cunningham will not be condemned before any Assize on Betty's word.'

Rob drew himself up and his voice went grim and flat. 'I know one that will condemn them, and I'll have them before it or my name is not Robert McGregor.' And from the look which fell across his face, Mary realized that there was no arguing.

That night, however, events were later to take on a darker and more desperate turn. Betty was in one of the outhouses, trying to make herself comfortable on the rough straw palliasse and staring up into the darkness. There was a gentle tap at the door and Mary came in, holding a storm lantern which flung grotesque shadows against the walls. 'Are you asleep?'

Betty shook her head. Mary was concerned. 'You must sleep, lass.'

Betty looked up at her, as if in a dwalm, 'I was thinking on Archie . . . I was thinking that, for all that has befallen me, if I heard his voice I would spring up and run to him . . . Am I not the sorriest creature you ever heard?' There was a kind of exhausted amazement in her voice.

Mary, ever practical, sat down, her hands covering Betty's. 'How does your bairn rest, Betty?'

'I wish it were me inside myself and not he, to tell you the truth.'

And Mary put her head against the girl's belly.

It was the last time she was to see Betty alive.

CHAPTER NINETEEN

You did all with your eyes

''Tis fit that we should do our part,
Becoming that mankind should learn
That we are not to be surpassed
In fatherly concern.'

Outside it was a wet and windy night. But, in the warmth of the front room of the tavern at Buchlyvie, Killearn was listening to the importuning and somewhat inebriated words of Argyll's erstwhile champion, Guthrie.

'The Englishman will never catch McGregor. Never at all. He knows nothing of the hills or the trails or the hidey-holes he has. Nothing! Put my name forward to His Lordship and I will find him. I swear to it.'

Suddenly from the back of the tavern came the unmistakable sound of cattle bellowing and the crash of furniture, mingled with the shouts and laughter of the patrons. Killearn went to the door and opened it. He could see that there were a few head of cattle trampling around in the main part of the bar, with more trying to force their way in. His first thought was of some high-spirited prank. 'What in the . . . ? If this is Cunningham . . .'

He was instantly disillusioned when a grunt from Guthrie made him swing round to see Rob, broadsword in hand, at the door of the bar. Killearn panicked and turned to bolt, but a steer had got in his way and instead he turned turtle in complete confusion, and somehow managed to force the door shut on the seemingly impassive Rob.

Killearn turned back to Guthrie in a dither of excitement. 'Now's your chance, Will, kill him . . . kill him!'

Guthrie unsheathed his sword as Rob kicked open the door and looked straight at Killearn without paying any heed to the other. 'This is not your fight, Guthrie. I'm here for Killearn.'

Instead, it was Guthrie who responded: 'And if I make it my fight?'

Rob looked at him in a manner which was nothing if not matter-of-fact. 'Then you'll be with Tam Sibbald in the morning.'

At this Guthrie hesitated, but Killearn, who was still tangled up with a brace or two of overexcited livestock, gathered sufficient wits to yell out: 'Take him, Will, and His Lordship will take you on, I warrant it.'

On these words the improvident Guthrie, knowing not how to avoid his allotted fate, raised his sword and lunged at Rob. It was a bad move, as Rob turned the blow aside and in a sweeping motion cut him deep and hard across the stomach, exposing the collops of his gut. Guthrie stared down at himself, unbelieving.

'My guts . . . !' He scarcely had time to look up as Rob stabbed him once, twice, through the chest, felling him for ever.

Killearn was staring, terrified, as Rob nonchalantly beckoned at him with his sword. Killearn gibbered, 'Don't kill me. It wasn't me.'

Rob was unimpressed. 'Outside, or I'll take an arm off you. The one you write with.'

Killearn scuttled around like a headless chicken until Rob took him by the scruff of the neck and firmly led him away. Outside the chaos continued, with the multitude of cattle around the tavern making any intervention or pursuit impossible.

Rob and Alasdair had Killearn prisoner in a small rowing-boat. Killearn was in the middle, anxiously gripping the gunwales, while Alasdair rowed in the bows behind him and Rob sat silent in the stern. Rob held a lantern which flickeringly showed Killearn's face. Killearn was dribbling at the mouth with fear. He was weighing up just how much Rob knew. As his ponderings swung in the balance, he had more than one bleak moment contemplating the dark waters by his side.

It was Killearn who eventually broke the silence. 'It's him the lass wants revenge on – Cunningham, and I grant he treated her sore.'

Rob was as silent and enigmatic as the glowering hills around the loch. Killearn shivered and took a look at where they were headed. Seeing the silhouette of a small island looming out of the darkness, he relaxed somewhat. However, turning back to Rob he was not exactly put at ease by the merciless gaze of the Highlander, but nevertheless unwisely blurted out: 'I gave no order at Craigrostan, all of that was his. The Englishman . . . your wife . . . she will tell you . . .'

He was met with more stony silence from Rob, but in desperation continued, 'If you harm me, His Lordship will hunt you down. You know it!'

Rob, who had been staring disconsolately down into the bilges, responded with a weary honesty which certainly did nothing to comfort the other man. 'I am past caring, Killearn.'

The boat ground ashore and the grating shingle somehow put a conclusive seal on the threat inherent in Rob's words.

There was a small deserted chapel on the island, almost hidden amongst a thicket of brambles and bracken. Rob and Alasdair casually pushed open the door and shoved Killearn inside, before carefully bolting it.

Rob turned to Alasdair. 'Fetch the lass and we'll try

him afore the morning.' Alasdair nodded and went back to the beach.

In the darkness, Killearn at first blundered around the chapel. Then, as the moon moved from behind a cloud, a shaft of light came down through a broken beam in the roof. It revealed the shadow of a perfectly formed noose hanging from a sturdy beam. Killearn called out in involuntary fright.

Inside the house at Rannoch, Mary was bustling about. After a while she turned to Alasdair, who was sitting glumly.

'I'll wake her. Treat her gentle, Alasdair, she's near the end of her tether,' and she went out carrying a lantern.

The boys were awake and Duncan looked up at Alasdair, 'Where's my father?'

Alasdair was silent as he went over to the pot of stew.

'Are the soldiers coming?' Ranald insisted.

Alasdair stared at them as he relished a piece of meat. 'You two should be sleeping.'

Mary went across the yard to the shed where Betty had settled down. She knocked, and getting no answer, pushed the door open and went in. Mary looked at where Betty had been lying asleep. It was vacant, and there was no sign of her in the room. Mary raised her lantern and looked around.

'Betty . . . ?'

Alasdair was still wolfing down his food in the kitchen

when the scream reached him. He got up, still stuffing food into his mouth, and headed for the door. The boys started to follow, but Alasdair turned on them sharply. 'Stay here.'

When Alasdair reached the shed he saw Mary desperately supporting Betty's body, which was hanging behind the door. As he rushed up to help take the weight he indicated the small dirk in his belt and yelled at Mary, 'Cut her down, quick . . .'

Mary released the weight into his arms, and grabbing the knife, furiously hacked at the rope around Betty's neck. The body eventually fell away and Alasdair carried it over to the litter. His gentleness notwithstanding, it was already too late, and it was clear to both of them that the girl was well dead.

On the following morning Rob was waiting on the island shore as Alasdair and Mary beached the boat.

'Mary, where is the girl?' he asked quietly.

Mary's face was a mask of desperate control, 'Betty Sturrock hanged herself in our shed.'

Rob stood for a moment recovering, before he turned back to Mary. 'Why are you here?'

Alasdair shuffled uncomfortably. 'She made me bring her. I told her—'

But Mary cut in quickly: 'I made him bring me, for I have dealings with this Killearn. I will confront this man, me and Betty Sturrock, and Betty Sturrock's child; the three of us will bring it out of him.'

Rob looked over at Alasdair who stared back at him,

giving nothing away. Mary seized the moment and grabbed Rob. Indicating Alasdair she held forth. 'This is no matter for him. It is between us. As I am your wife, Robert, I will have my way in this . . . I will.' Confronted by such conviction, Rob could only slowly nod.

Inside the ruined chapel, Killearn, who had been sleeping fitfully, slowly came awake and tried to discern the figures in the doorway.

'Betty, is that you?'

Mary was not slow to respond. 'Betty is dead. She killed herself this night – and her unborn with her . . .'

Killearn got up, recognizing the voice. 'Mistress McGregor . . . so the poor girl is dead?'

'Spare me your hypocrisy, Killearn. You are as much her murderer as she – you and that Englishman.'

'I had no part in her child, any more than the matter at Craigrostan.'

Mary advanced, her voice lowering. 'You stood and gloated; you did all with your eyes.'

Suddenly the wily Killearn sensed a possible chink of hope in her conspiratorial tone and asked, 'Yet you have not told him . . . ?' He looked at her, assessing the situation.

'Do you think me such a puppet that I would put my husband's head in a noose fashioned from my own dishonour?'

Killearn was beginning to feel more confident. 'You have a proposal for me, I can tell.'

'You will sign your name to a statement telling how you slew Alan McDonald, stole my husband's money and burned our property. Before a judge you will sign it.'

Killearn was dismissive. 'And he will hang me at the Tolbooth for my trouble. No great inducement, Mistress McGregor.'

They were very close now, almost like plotters, as Mary tried to hold together her unravelling scheme.

'When it is signed, you may go where you will, where you can.'

Killearn came back at her, his eyes gleaming in mock admiration. 'I will not soon forget the last time I saw you, Mary, how nobly you walked from that burning – like a queen.'

The words entered her like a knife, and she stiffened and backed away. 'You will agree to this, or else.'

Killearn now felt he might just have gained the upper hand. 'Or else what . . . ? You will tell Rob how Cunningham used you?'

He saw from the look in her eyes that, indeed, he did have the advantage and he pressed it home. '. . . I have another picture, not so noble, of you stood in Lomond water washing between your legs.'

Mary was now backed up against the table as Killearn bore down on her and continued relentlessly: '. . . Did you wash it out, or, did the Englishman colonize another Scottish—'

She hit him a sudden stinging blow across the face, but he shrugged it off and went on. 'I have a proposal for you, Mistress McGregor. Convince your man that Cunningham alone killed his man, and he did, and kept the money entirely, which he did, and I will not speak of what you might have inside you.'

He nudged her with his belly, an obscene prodding which drove her further back against the table. '. . . Rob would be hard pressed to love such a bastard, would he not?'

He saw that he had struck home and that Mary could not gainsay this. He smiled in triumph. 'But you know the saying, Mary, "'Tis a wise father knows his own child". If you'll not tell, neither will I.'

But Killearn would have been wiser not to have rubbed the point in, for out of nowhere came a hand with a knife in it – the very knife that had cut down the hapless Betty – as Mary stabbed him in the throat leaving a jagged wound that gouted large gobbets of blood over the dusty chapel floor. Killearn emitted a strangled, gurgling cry as he staggered back, and Mary stared straight into his amazed eyes.

'You have my word on it.'

Killearn bolted for the door with his hands clutching his throat. As he burst into the open, Rob and Alasdair stared at him in surprise and horror. As Killearn ran through the trees, blood pumping through his clenched fingers, Rob leapt up and sprinted into the chapel. 'Mary! Are you harmed?'

She shook her head slowly as he continued, '. . . What have you done, woman; woman, what have you done?' Then he saw the knife, shiny silver and glistening with red.

At the side of the loch, Killearn was kneeling in the

water staring at the blood as Alasdair came up behind him. 'She cut me.'

Alasdair was unimpressed. 'Not deep enough for me.' Calmly he took hold of Killearn's scalp and held the head under the water. The blood pulsed out freely before mingling in and getting lost with the waters of the loch. Patiently, almost absent-mindedly, Alasdair held the head under while the struggle slackened and eventually subsided.

Inside the chapel, Mary, her face puffed out with the effects of shock, stared at the knife. Rob was uneasy, for he thought he knew Mary, and there was something untoward going on here. 'Mary, what brought you to such a thing?'

'He needed killing and I was as fit to do it as you.'

Rob was thoughtful for a moment. 'That's no answer.'

Mary looked round and realized she could keep up the concealment no longer. 'There is more to it.'

'Aye, like enough . . .' Rob did not allow himself to betray any surprise.

Mary caught his arm. 'Sit, Robert, I must tell you the reasons.'

'Sit! There's no sitting now.'

At this Alasdair came in. 'He's gone, gutted and sunk.'

Mary shuddered and was suddenly silent. Rob, anxious to be gone, grabbed up the dirk and tossed it at Alasdair with a black look. 'Best you had kept that about you . . .' Turning back to Mary, he put a hand on her shoulder. 'Come, Mary, we must pack the lads and flee.'

CHAPTER TWENTY

And he'll be a dear one, I'm thinking

'Of old things all are over old,
Of good things none are good enough:
We'll show that we can help to frame
A world of other stuff.'

Inside Montrose's office, things were not going too cheerily for the hapless Cunningham. Montrose was splenetic with rage.

'I am mocked by this rogue that you undertook to deliver me as broken!'

Cunningham, reaching wildly for something to say, began falteringly, 'Your Lordship—'

But Montrose would have none of it. 'Do not, do not I say, speak in my stead. Damn you sir, but there is more here than I see. Killearn and you have some hand in matters hid from sight . . .' And he fingered the lapel of

Cunningham's coat, a gaudy, figured affair of silk and brocade. 'This tells me you are in cash – and I know you are without means.'

Cunningham chanced his arm weakly with a rather unconvincing attempt at nonchalance. 'Gaming, Your Lordship; the cards favoured . . .'

At this Montrose erupted, 'Do you take me entirely for a wig, sir?' He leaned in on Cunningham's face, vicious and compelling. '. . . I care not what you and that greasy capon cooked up. But put an end to this impudence against me, or God, sir, you were best where Killearn is now.'

Cunningham was silent. He could see that he had finally come to the end of his master's tether.

As the flames rose from the thatch of Rob and Mary's bolt-hole at Rannoch, the troopers continued to throw the few items of furniture on the roof in a desultory attempt to keep the fire going. Others were milling about in a half-hearted search for plunder. Cunningham, however, set-faced, was riding up and down trying desperately to comport himself like a conqueror.

Behind the house, where the hills went steeply up to the cloud-covered ridge, Rob, Alasdair and Coll, with a few others of the Gregorach, lay behind some rocks and looked down into the valley. Alasdair, who had been a little way off, crawled over to Rob and Coll. He had a musket on his back.

'We can't let them burn, loot and ride away. We should hit them, Rob.'

Rob didn't look at him, but the younger man continued: 'Cunningham, he's there, on the white horse. He's the one who took Craigrostan.'

Rob replied tersely, 'I know fine who he is.'

Alasdair pressed on: 'Have you no thought to avenge Mary for that?'

Rob looked over at Alasdair, puzzled, as Coll interjected, 'There's thirty or more – and mounted, man . . . they'd ride us down like sheep.'

Alasdair was appalled. 'Alasdair McGregor is no sheep.'

But Rob was more realistic. 'Coll's right. We can do nothing'

He got to his feet and started to move up the slope while the others, with the exception of Alasdair, got up too. Alasdair nursed his musket for a moment before making as if to follow.

Far beneath them, the pillage was complete and Cunningham called his troop together while the thatch was left to burn itself out. Suddenly, as they were preparing to ride away, a shot rang out and one of the men was killed from the back of his horse. Mindful of their training, the others immediately scattered and took what cover they could behind the burning buildings. Only Cunningham was unstirred, riding forward to gaze up the glen.

Alasdair rose from his ill-considered shot with triumph on his face. 'A hit . . . a hit.'

Rob and the others stopped and looked back in disbelief as Rob muttered under his breath, 'Damn the fool.'

From below, Cunningham, alerted by the puff of blue smoke, had spotted Alasdair halfway up the slope. He called to his men and spurred his horse forward. The troopers emerged from their cover and started up the hill behind him. The Gregorach, seeing them break out into the open, pressed on desperately to attain the safety of the ridge. Alasdair stood a moment longer, yelling defiance, before he too turned and ran.

Rob waited as Alasdair caught up with him. 'I hit one of them.'

Rob nodded. 'Aye, and he'll be a dear one, I'm thinking.'

And the two of them started up the hill to the cover of the cloud.

Behind them, the troopers were forcing their horses at the slope – spurring them and beating their flanks with the flats of their swords. The mist cleared for a moment and Cunningham ordered some of them to dismount and take fire at a group of the Gregorach who were barely fifty yards ahead. Rob and Alasdair were the rearmost of the fleeing group. As the shots began to sing around them, Rob turned round: 'Damn you, Alasdair, for a fool.'

Alasdair, however, seemed to be enjoying himself and looked over at the older man. 'You're getting too old for the wars, Rob. What will you do when the King comes?'

But it was a short-lived moment of triumph. Before Rob could respond, Alasdair was suddenly pitched forward, stumbling to his knees, struck in the back by a musket ball. He struggled to get up but crumpled in a heap, and Rob quickly rolled him up on to his shoulder and kept on running.

Cunningham could see that one of them was hit, and called out again to his men to follow as he spurred his own horse on. The first of the Gregorach had by now reached the safety of the cloud-line, disappearing into the murk like phantoms. Before following suit, Coll stopped to look back for a moment. He could see Rob labouring up the steep slope with Alasdair on his back, the horsemen now gaining rapidly.

'Run, Rob, run for yourself . . .' but before Coll could finish his words, he was hit in the stomach and fell back in the heather with a groan.

Rob was starting to slow down. The cloud-line was still some distance off and he could hear the pounding of hoofs as the troopers galloped up behind him.

Alasdair, realizing his blame in the matter, started to protest. 'Put me down . . . I can run . . .'

But Rob merely replied, 'Shut your mouth,' and renewed his efforts as he ploughed on up the slope.

He must have found an unexpected reserve of strength in himself, because Cunningham could see that Rob was just going to make it into the cloud in time and ordered another volley. The men pulled up and leapt off, the air suddenly crackling with the volley from their heavy horse pistols.

Rob and Alasdair struggled safely into the cloud but further along the hillside Coll was struggling to his feet.

He was hit again in the fresh volley, and this time when he fell he was dead.

Rob looked back momentarily just as the cloud obscured the horsemen. In a last desperate burst of speed, with Alasdair still on his back, he headed off on a long diagonal across the ridge, hoping to outflank the horsemen and believing that, so long as he was not spotted, they would continue straight up the hillside.

Cunningham and his troopers came charging into the mist. At once they were enveloped and almost on top of each other in the confusion. Furiously, Cunningham ordered them to spread out and refrain from using their pistols.

'Sabre them. Cut them down.'

Further along the hillside, Rob was now on his hands and knees, Alasdair sprawled along his back. Grimly he crawled on up the slope, the thudding of hoofs faintly reaching him through his palms. Alasdair groaned and whispered, 'Let me lie till I get my wind, Rob . . . That thing knocked the breath out of me.' But Rob paid him no heed – just silently kept on crawling.

Suddenly he saw a great dark shape looming up in front of them. He threw Alasdair clear, and dragging his sword free was on his feet, only to realize that the shape was a standing stone. A few yards off he could just discern the faint outline of another. Gasping with relief, he went over to Alasdair and dragged him to the base of the stone. He turned, breathless, and looked around him in the swirling mist for a few moments. There was no sign of their pursuers.

He bent down to take a look at Alasdair's wound, leaning over to get at his back. 'Hold still.'

He could see where Alasdair was hit, just below the shoulder-blade. Alasdair groaned again, 'Knocked the breath out of me.' Rob was in no doubts as to just how serious it was as he lay Alasdair back against the stone and turned once again to scan the mist.

'I cannot feel my legs, Rob. Are they there?'

Rob was silent as he watched a couple of riders loom briefly out of the mist before disappearing again. He turned back to Alasdair. 'Aye, your legs are fine.'

But through his delirium, Alasdair knew he was dying and that there was something he must explain before it was too late. 'Forgive me, Rob, for I should have told you . . .'

'Save your breath, lad.'

Alasdair was sinking fast and rambling now. 'She made me swear silence, I did not want to . . .'

He passed out for a moment, but with a struggle opened his eyes again. 'Lift me up, Rob. She said if she could bear it to be done – lift me up, Rob, so I can see you again . . . If she could bear it, so must I . . .'

Rob tried to lift him up. 'Bear what?' And Rob pulled him further up against the side of the stone.

'How they used her.'

'Who used her?' Suddenly, and at last, Rob's mind was focused on what Alasdair was trying to tell him.

'She would not tell you for fear . . . Rob, I cannot see you.'

'I'm here.'

Alasdair's vision was fading, but Rob was now listening urgently, desperate for the information. '. . . Alasdair, Alasdair, what of Mary, what of it . . . ?'

With a final effort, Alasdair managed to get the words out. 'They violated her. She would not tell you, to spare you the grief.'

Rob knew what it was that he was being told, and it crushed all else for a moment. He stared into Alasdair's eyes which were fast glazing over, and almost shook him. 'Who? Who did this?'

Chapter Twenty-One

Broken but not dead

'I too, will have my kings that take
From me the sign of life and death:
Kingdoms shall shift about, like clouds,
Obedient to my breath.'

Some twenty yards or so from the circle of standing stones, Cunningham was standing up in his stirrups and staring around. The mist was beginning to thin slightly and he could now make out the shapes of the stones. More and more of his horsemen began to appear, and one of them came riding up, dragging Coll's body along the ground by a rope, and made his report. 'We have one of them.'

Another of the troopers joined them. 'The rest have gone to earth.'

Over at the stones themselves, Alasdair was trying to

pull himself upright against the side of one of them. Rob, who was crouching stock-still and, aware that the mist was thinning, had been straining every nerve to follow the horsemen's movements, didn't realize this until Alasdair's hand brushed against his shoulder. He started and jerked round to see Alasdair's hands clamped to the stone.

'Alasdair! Stand still.'

But Alasdair was in a world of his own and simply kept trying to pull himself up the stone, his useless legs dangling behind him.

The mist had by now almost completely gone, and Rob could clearly see several horsemen gathering together as if they were getting ready to make their way back down the hillside. He was just about to try and drag Alasdair back, when one of the troopers spotted the desperate figure breaking above the silhouette of the stone. The horseman came riding up and when he was within point-blank range, dispatched Alasdair with a single shot from his pistol. Although Alasdair was quite dead, such had been his final determination that he did not fall, but hung instead from the top of the stone, his hands clenched on it as if it were life itself.

The horseman came to investigate, but before he could even dismount, Rob had stepped from behind the stone and driven his sword up through the trooper's ribs. As the horseman fell back, Rob seized the reins and hauled himself into the saddle. The single shot had alerted the other troopers, and Rob could see them approaching as he struggled to disentangle one of the stricken man's feet from the stirrup.

Rob tried to kick the horse into a canter, but the body of the trooper dragged alongside making the horse shy and veer off to the side. When the dead man eventually did fall away the troopers were almost up with the horse. Rob kicked the horse and at last it began to gallop. He crouched low, heading for a narrow glen where there were still a few patches of thick cloud.

When the inevitable shot did ring out it was not Rob who was hit. Instead, the ball buried itself in the horse's flank, pitching it forward and throwing the rider over its head. Rob thudded to the ground and was instantly knocked unconscious.

As Rob eventually came to, the first thing he was aware of was the face of Cunningham coolly surveying his trophy and smirking.

'Well, well, if it's not the great McGregor – come to hand at last.'

It was a matter of minutes to bind Rob's wrists together and attach them with a length of rope to the pommel of Cunningham's saddle. To either side of him, the bodies of Coll and Alasdair were roped by their feet to Cunningham's horse so that they dragged along the ground. Despite the extra load, Cunningham set off at a brisk canter and Rob was scarcely able to keep his feet. After one particularly bad stumble Cunningham turned to him.

'I see you have not travelled in this fashion before . . . never mind, I wager you will master it before nightfall.'

That night, when they finally stopped and prepared to set up camp, Rob's feet were bound together and he was dumped by the roadside next to where the horses were hobbled. He was covered in mud and bruises from the many falls he had sustained along the way. Although it was not particularly cold, he shivered convulsively from shock. He had tried straining at his bonds, but it was pointless. They were wickedly tight.

The camp was settling down for the night and Rob could see the troopers huddling around their fires, when Cunningham came up. He approached to within a few feet of his prisoner and stopped.

'Well, McGregor, how does it seem to you tonight . . . Is God's great plan for us all to your liking?'

Rob said nothing, but merely stared at his tormentor, who gloated for a moment and then continued.

'"Broken but not dead" was His Lordship's request. I will do my part, if you will do yours, and not die before the bridge at Glen Orchy.'

Still there was no response from Rob, and Cunningham leaned over closer and inquired, almost confidentially, '. . . Tell me, what did you do with that bag of guts, Killearn?'

Rob remained silent, and this was beginning to annoy Cunningham, who cuffed him over the head.

'. . . Vex me not, McGregor, or I shall have you dragged awhile . . . and I am a man of my word.'

When Rob eventually did speak it was with a bitter strength. 'You are a thief, a murderer, a betrayer and a violator of women.'

Cunningham's eyes lit up at this last point. 'I had hoped you would have come to me long since on that score.'

'Had I known earlier, you would be dead sooner.'

This rankled Cunningham, and he leaned close in on Rob's face. 'I will tell you something to take with you. Your wife was sweeter forced than many are willing – in truth, put to it, I think not all of her objected.'

Rob's lunge upward at his throat almost took him by surprise, but he jerked back just in time as Rob's teeth closed harmlessly on his collar. Although his neck was clear, the sheer animal ferocity of the move had Cunningham in a panic, trying to pull back as he beat Rob with his fists. Rob's clenched jaw hung on as Cunningham backed away, dragging him until the material tore loose and Cunningham sprang up. He touched the torn collar and pondered its proximity to his throat.

Then he turned on the bound man and started to kick him. Rob merely glared back, the piece of severed material still between his teeth.

Inside his ramshackle hall, Argyll was standing with his back to a huge hearth, a crew of wolfish-looking deer-hounds sprawled at his feet. Mary was sitting on a low chair before him. Argyll was thoughtful and chose his words with care. 'I appreciate the honour you do me,

Mistress McGregor, in bringing your case, but from all I am acquainted with your husband, he has earned the enmity of the Marquis of Montrose by borrowing money that he cannot repay – and ever harrying his stock as blackmail.'

Mary replied respectfully, 'There is more to the matter, Your Grace.'

'I am sure there is, but it is not part of mine to intrude myself, sensible though I am to your condition. It is a hard truth, but men make the quarrels and women and weans bear them.'

Mary came to what she hoped was her trump card. 'Your Grace, Robert finds himself in this condition for taking your part.'

Argyll was more puzzled now. 'My part? What cause had he to do that – and in what manner . . . ?'

Mary was now hopeful that he would hear her out. 'He refused to condemn you by false witness when the Marquis asked him to say you were a Jacobite, to injure your name at Court.'

'Montrose asked this of him?' Argyll asked gently.

Mary pressed on, becoming breathless: 'In remission of this debt. But Robert refused.'

Argyll pondered this for a moment, not quite sure whether to believe it or not. 'I did not know your husband bore me such goodwill.'

Mary was nothing if not matter-of-fact. 'Indeed, Your Grace, I think he favours you no more than any other great man. "As wolves at lambing", is his word for you all.'

Argyll could hear in her voice the great respect she held for her husband, and how even now, in her moment of need, she would not betray his wish never to be misrepresented. Argyll listened attentively as she continued, guilelessly: '. . . It was done not for Your Grace, but for his own honour, which he holds dearer than myself or his sons, his clan or his kin, and for which I have oft chided him. But it is him and his way, and were he other, he would not be Robert Roy McGregor.'

She paused and drew breath as Argyll remained silent. 'He would not come here before you, nor would he favour me to do so in his stead, but I have no choice unless I give him up entire to his enemies, and though I love his honour, it is but a moon-cast shadow to the love I bear him. For by God's Grace, I have his child in me . . . and I would have a father for it.'

Argyll pondered this for a moment, then nodded solemnly. 'You do your man no dishonour, Mary. Faith, he is a man much blessed by fortune.'

CHAPTER TWENTY-TWO

At the Bridge of Glen Orchy

And if the word had been fulfilled,
As might *have been, then, thought of joy!*
France would have had her present Boast,
And we our own Rob Roy!

On the following morning, Rob was once again roped to Cunningham's saddle. Exhausted, his face was now a mask of caked blood and raised bruises. Now mindful of his prisoner's teeth, Cunningham had had him gagged with a stick between his teeth and tied back behind his head. His arms and legs were raw, and he was moving with reserves of will which came from he knew not where. Slowly they climbed the long slope up towards the bridge over the Tulla burn at Glen Orchy.

Montrose and his entourage were waiting for them

there as arranged. A small pavilion had been set up and Montrose was within, enjoying a civilized breakfast as his men waited outside, milling around and stamping, in vain attempts to keep warm in the chill, damp air. Their breath billowed around, grey skeins in the murky light of the early dawn.

A lookout on horseback spied Cunningham's party, and waiting only for a moment before he turned his horse around, he wheeled back over the bridge. He dismounted and entered Montrose's temporary shelter. Montrose looked up impassively.

'They are coming, my Lord.'

'And have they my man?'

'They are dragging something like . . .' But at this the man tailed off.

On hearing these words, Montrose, resplendent in a great fur-trimmed cape and a freshly powdered wig, strode out on to the bridge to watch the cavalcade ride up. It came to a halt in front of him, Cunningham at its head. As he reigned in, Rob was jerked to a halt, staggered and collapsed to his knees. He stayed there unable to move. Cunningham smirked. 'Broken, but not dead, Your Lordship. At your request.'

Montrose came over to look at his prize. Cunningham dismounted and jerked up Rob's bowed head. Montrose flinched a little at the shock of the sight. Seeing this, Cunningham sought to explain the gag.

'A precaution against his teeth. The man is more animal than human.'

Montrose seemed more irritable than pleased. 'Cut it

loose. I would have him tell me what he has done with Killearn.'

Cunningham was suddenly defensive. 'I questioned him to the point, but he would admit nothing.'

Montrose snapped out: 'Ungag him now and I will ask my own questions.'

Cunningham nodded and made a sign to one of his men, who cut the cords and pulled the stick out of Rob's mouth, which was now deformed into a terrible rictus which bled freely. Montrose looked at him. 'So, McGregor, what have you to say for yourself . . . ?'

With an effort Rob hauled himself to his feet, working his mouth to slacken the jaw. Rob regarded him for a moment and then spoke thickly, his mouth still half-paralysed.

'I am wronged by His Lordship.' He paused to spit bloodily before continuing with a sideways glance at Cunningham, 'And by those who serve him.'

Montrose's response was explosive. 'You are wronged? You? Unless I am much mistaken, 'tis myself who is short a thousand pound, whose cattle are reived, whose factor, Killearn, is abducted . . .'

Rob nodded at Cunningham. 'Ask this thing where your money is, and where he sunk Alan McDonald after he killed him.'

Montrose looked shrewdly at Rob for a moment and then turned to Cunningham, who shrugged.

'The same accusation he spat at me; desperate words from a desperate man.'

Montrose turned again to Rob. 'You have proofs of these matters?'

Rob looked him straight in the eye. 'You have my word on it.'

The words came out without a trace of bravado nor indeed any particular emphasis. For a moment, Montrose was in the thrall of the Highlander's simple honesty and unwavering gaze. Montrose was silent, then as if shaking himself free of the spell, looked down and spoke quietly.

'I think it will take more than that.'

Rob indicated Cunningham. 'Then you have the nature of this man here. If you cannot tell what is true from what is not, I fear Your Lordship's judgement is past repairing.'

Cunningham hit him a blow to the side of the head which sent Rob staggering, and he dropped to his knees once again. Montrose looked at him, loathing and also a sort of sad world-weariness in his eyes.

'Hang him from the bridge.'

Cunningham turned back to his mount, loosened the rope from the saddle and threw it down on the ground. As Montrose turned away, Cunningham could not resist a final taunt and, taking care not to get too close, yelled out: 'You'll piss but you won't whistle this time, McGregor.'

But as he turned away he failed to see his foolish error as Rob, in a flash, gathered up the loose end of the rope and threw a loop of it around Cunningham's head. Jerking it tight, Rob jumped over the low parapet of the bridge, dragging Cunningham with him and wedging him against the parapet. Rob dangled beneath the bridge with his weight supported, ultimately, by Cunningham's neck.

As the rope cut into the flesh, it seemed for a moment that it would strangle Cunningham until one of the troopers leapt forward and severed the cord with a single blow. Cunningham slumped down on the roadway of the bridge, gagging and choking, as Rob dropped into the rushing water below and was twenty yards downstream before anyone could move.

Montrose stared at Cunningham for a brief moment, his eyes anything but sympathetic. Then he swung on the gawking men and pointed at Rob.

'There he is, there . . . I want him back.'

As the troopers ran to their mounts, Cunningham got to his feet unsteadily, rage and disappointment welling up through the shock of his near garotting. He attempted to regain the initiative by shouting out orders but at once found that nothing would come out of his mouth. Instead, he ran to his horse and was quickly among the troopers trying to find a way off the bridge and down on to the bank.

Rob was carried along in the current, his hands still tied together in front of him. The water was fast and cold as he was swept along, trying to avoid the snags and rocks in the bank.

Cunningham and the troopers had by now found a way down, and they started along the bank. Rob was still out of their sight, but on horseback they rapidly began to make up the distance.

The river was suddenly flowing faster through steeper, narrower banks. Rob managed to look ahead for a moment where it dropped down into a small gorge. There was the sound of a waterfall – a numbing, roaring noise – and he prepared himself as best he could for the passage.

Abruptly he was brought up short by the submerged branch of a fallen tree. It fetched him a terrible blow in the ribs. Worse, the pressure of the current held him there, unable to extricate himself. He hung there, the water breaking over him, and looked back through the alders at the first of the troopers working his way along the bank. Some way behind he could just see Cunningham standing up in the stirrups, still voiceless but conveying his emotions well enough in a look of demoniacal rage.

In the river, Rob was growing desperate and weary from trying to free himself. Finally he managed to break the branch without disengaging it from his clothing, but by now he was all too aware that the horsemen would be on him in seconds.

Then, under the bank, he saw a dark shape. It was the carcass of a cow, burst open and bloated, its insides exposed. He dragged himself along until he reached it.

Its interior was a cavern of putrefaction, and he gagged as for a moment his whole being was revulsed at the sight, but then he heard the shouts of his pursuers growing closer and he pushed himself up into the fetid interior, twisting himself along the animal's spine.

He lay there holding his breath and shuddering as

Cunningham and the troopers passed along the bank above him.

The troopers went on downstream to where the river rushed between narrow walls, and plunged in a welter of foam over the rocks and into a deep pool. It was a waterfall which seemed sufficiently daunting for them to rein in nervously and scan the banks on either side for a body. Cunningham stared down into the dark water at the foot of the fall. One of his men came up and followed his gaze.

'He's dead if he went down there.'

Cunningham stared at him and tried to order him to go down, but his voice did not respond. Instead he pointed down, angrily stabbing his finger at the pool, with strange croaking sounds emanating weakly from him.

Dismounting, the trooper started down to search the scrub and bracken of the bank. The others followed him down while Cunningham clutched at his throat and rode up and down in a frenzy of frustration.

Rob lay in the carcass, enduring its horrors as his pursuers beat up and down the shallows and now began to retrace the way they had come. He was staring into a slow pulsation of maggots a few inches from his nose, his face set in a grimace.

The nearest they ever came to him was when he heard a voice asking what the stink was, and then heard the dead cow being identified. Satisfied with this they came no closer, and began to wander off while Rob briefly passed into a kind of coma of exhaustion and shock.

[illegible] and the troopers [illegible]

The troopers were [illegible] where the [illegible]

[illegible]

Chapter Twenty-Three

It is not the child who needs killing

Oh! say not so; compare them not;
I would not wrong thee, Champion brave!
Would wrong thee nowhere; least of all
Here standing by thy grave.

Mary, Ranald and Duncan were once again in a small cart making their way towards a new home. It was a pleasant, simple stone house set by a burn and with a tree beside the door. The burn ran on down the valley towards the loch shining in the distance between steep hills.

Ranald was the first to break the silence. 'Is this where we may stay?'

Mary looked at him and nodded. 'Aye, by the goodness of His Grace, under his protection.'

Duncan perked up, 'And father? . . . Will he come here?'

Mary dismounted gingerly. 'If he can . . .' And they started to unload the cart.

At their *clachan* the Gregorach were standing around outside their cottages, men, women and children alike, as Cunningham and his troops searched and ransacked the interiors. The bodies of Alasdair and Coll lay beside the track where they had been casually dumped.

Cunningham was only really looking for Rob, and when he was satisfied that he was not there, ordered the troopers to mount and led them out.

The Gregorach gathered round their dead, their grief rising.

The house was quiet and dark when Rob slipped up to it. Mary was asleep, but something made her stir and she woke. Meaning to go and check on the boys, she was half up when she saw Rob sitting hunched against the wall like an apparition, staring into the dim glow of the peats. She scrambled up in a panic of disbelief and was at his side in an instant.

'Robert, oh my Robert, I had thought you . . .' And then she saw the state of him and the hollow, drained look in his face and her tone changed. '. . . What have they done with you . . .' She took his hands, delicately touched his face, put her arms around him and felt him flinch with the pain, and then she drew back. For the first time he looked at her.

'You should have told me, Mary.' The words were

uttered not in reproach, but with a terrible flat regret which cut her to the heart.

'Oh, Robert, I could not. I should have, but I could not . . .' She could see him looking at her for a moment and then instantly away. Stung by her feelings of guilt she went on, 'Forgive me my love, I was wrong, it was wrong.'

He shook his head. 'It was me who was wrong . . .'

He looked at her properly now, almost pleading: 'You said right when you told me I must have it my own way. It's that which brought all this on us.'

Mary wanted to stop this bout of self-accusation, but Rob was looking away again. '. . . I should have packed my pride and given Montrose his way.'

Mary shook her head quickly, 'No, Robert.'

Rob looked around. 'And all this that has come on us, all this you have endured.'

He stopped, as if unable to voice it all, and looked again at Mary, who continued, 'No, no, Rob.'

But his voice strengthened as he went on. 'Yes, Mary. Craigrostan would still be ours. Alasdair and Coll would be alive.'

'And wrong would have been done you . . .'

'And what of the wrong done you, wrong past bearing?'

She took his hands. 'Not past bearing, not if I have my Robert and he has himself – and you would not, not if you had done a lesser man's bidding. Honour is the gift a man gives himself. You told our boys so. Would you have stolen from yourself what makes you Robert

McGregor?' She was breathing renewed life into him with these words, by her eyes on him, by her love of him, and he responded to it.

'Oh, my Mary, how fine you are to me.'

Mary replied, 'And you to me.'

She kissed him and he closed his eyes and lay back. They lay there together for a timeless moment, but then Mary stopped and looked at him. He looked back, and the first ghost of a smile came to his eyes.

With an enormous effort of will Mary blurted out, 'There is more.' Rob started, suddenly fearing worse but unable to imagine it. He stared at her, childlike.

'What more?'

Mary went on into the unknown. 'I am carrying a child . . . and I do not know who the father is.' It almost broke her to say it – and him to hear it. His hand fell away, not in rejection, simply in collapse. He sat for a moment, strangely shrunken, all manner of mysteries now becoming painfully clear.

'Ach Mary . . . Mary . . .'

She watched him, waiting for him to continue, but he said nothing.

'I could not kill it, husband . . .'

He held up a hand, cutting her off, and she fell silent. Then from the bottom of his soul came the words, 'It is not the child who needs killing, Mary.'

Chapter Twenty-Four

There are more than champions here

For Thou, although with some wild thoughts,
Wild Chieftain of a savage Clan!
Hadst this to boast of; thou didst love
The liberty *of man.*

Argyll was in his chamber, staring at the tall gaunt figure standing before him, and slowly shook his head doubtfully. 'This point of honour might likely kill you, sir. I have seen the man at work, and he is no dunce with a blade.'

Rob, for the tall man was none other, simply replied: 'If Your Lordship could arrange it, I would be even more in his debt than I presently stand.'

It was an evasive, inflexible response, and Argyll studied the man for a moment, then, his mind made up, curtly nodded. 'Very well. I will see what I can make of it.'

Rob gave a short bow and turned to go, but Argyll called him back. 'McGregor!' and as Rob paused: '. . . He will kill you, McGregor. I would lose money if I wagered other.'

Rob turned towards Argyll. 'Your Lordship has my permission to profit in whatever way he may.' And he strode out, leaving the older man to make what he might out of this implied rebuke.

In the garden at Montrose's, Cunningham, his neck heavily swathed in bandages, sat by a flower-bed gazing in a wistful kind of way at the miniature portrait of his mother. Hearing a noise, he looked up and saw Montrose heading towards him. He rose and put the miniature away.

Montrose came straight to the point. 'I have had a correspondence from His Grace, the Duke of Argyll. It would seem our McGregor is holed with him.'

Cunningham waited. He was still having difficulty speaking. Montrose continued, 'He offers us a match . . .'

Cunningham's hand went to his throat, but Montrose, not expecting a vocal answer, pressed on. '. . . You and the Highlander. Argyll would recoup his loss on his last wager.'

At last Cunningham managed a few words. 'Bring him on.'

The words were like broken glass in his throat. At this Montrose started, stared at him in amazement and then exclaimed: 'You speak, Archibald!' Shaking his head he went off muttering to himself, 'One must never underestimate the healing power of hatred.'

Inside Argyll's cottage at Glen Shirra Rob was standing, stripped to the waist, with his arms raised. The bruises and scrapes to his upper torso were still clearly visible as Mary wound a long strip of linen around him. Ranald and Duncan watched as he winced against the pressure, their faces involuntarily miming his discomfort. Mary's face was drawn with apprehension at the conversation that was taking place.

Duncan insisted, 'But how long must you go, Father?'

'Just a while.'

It was Ranald's turn. 'Is it business you have with the Duke?'

Mary finished her binding and Rob lowered his arms.

'Aye, business.' He put on his shirt and, seeking to change the subject, went on: 'Have you noticed, lads, that we have another among us?' They looked at him, and Mary reacted as Rob put a hand on her body. 'Show them where it's hid, Mary.'

The boys looked at her and began to realize what was meant. Mary looked back at them, a little embarrassed as they drew closer. Duncan was the bolder. 'Is it inside you?'

She nodded. Rob picked up his gear, and looked at the three of them. His face was touched by the emotions of the moment. Seeing this, Mary looked back at him.

The moment was soon broken and gone when Ranald asked, 'How does it get out?'

Rob grinned, 'Same road it got in.' Which didn't leave them much the wiser as he headed for the door. Mary gestured to the boys to stay, and followed him out.

Above the house on the hill behind, Argyll's men were waiting. Rob was looking up at them as Mary came out and caught hold of him. He turned and held her to him tightly.

'Rob, what if—'

'Wheesht.'

But she shook her head and persisted, 'I cannot . . . What if you do not return to us?'

Rob looked down on her. 'If he is a boy, call him Robert. And if a lass, name her for my love, Mary McGregor.' He kissed her once and was gone by the time the boys had joined Mary at the door. They hardly saw him go, as he was already striding up the hillside to join the other men.

Argyll was at the head of the column with Rob beside him, as they made their way to the scene of the challenge. Rob was still suffering from his wounds and rode with controlled but obvious discomfort. Argyll looked at Rob with curiosity and not a little concern as they jolted along.

At length Argyll spoke. 'My man Guthrie was like an ox at the knacker's yard under Cunningham's blade. You will need to be twice as quick as poor Will.' Rob said nothing but merely continued to jolt along impassively. Argyll decided to try another tack. 'Tell me, is this matter of honour concerning your wife . . . ?'

Rob replied without any obvious emotion: 'It is concerning me, Your Grace. Mr Cunningham and I have matters outstanding.'

Argyll perceived that he had got somewhere close to the truth. 'She will not thank you for making her a widow, honour or no.'

Rob looked over at him. 'Perhaps Your Grace will wager a sum for her maintenance?'

Argyll wondered if he was serious, but there was no way of knowing. 'If it will help you die any the easier, I'll lay twenty guineas for her.'

Rob glanced back. 'Fifty would go further.'

Argyll appreciated this, and laughingly slapped him on the shoulder, which caused Rob to gasp in pain. 'By God, but you have a style to you. "Wolves at lambing". I liked that.'

After this they rode on in a grim silence.

Well ahead of the appointed time the hall was packed and loud with the hubbub of expectation. Montrose was already there and Cunningham with him, as Argyll and Rob entered. As they strode in, the babble of conversation rose to a new level.

Without any formality, Rob went over to the sword cabinets and stood silently contemplating the range and variety of the weaponry. Argyll headed straight for Montrose, ignoring Cunningham who was staring malevolently at Rob's back.

Montrose was the first to speak, stiffly formal: 'So,

what are we to wager on this outcome, Your Grace? . . . Guineas again . . . ?'

'I want no part of this. There are more than champions here. I think these men hate each other.'

Montrose glanced over at the two of them. 'Aye, they are not overfond.'

Rob had chosen his weapon, a traditional heavy basket-handled broadsword, and was making a few experimental swings to assess its weight and balance. For his part, Cunningham was ready. Stripped down, he made a lethal figure, spare as a blade and sparkling with malice.

Argyll confronted Montrose. 'You offered McGregor amnesty from his debts if he would lay charges against me.'

Montrose stared back at him poker-faced. 'Is that how he cozened you to give him shelter?'

'I know the truth when I hear it.'

Montrose smirked, 'And here was me thinking that was God's gift alone.'

Rankling at this stylish cynicism, Argyll suddenly forced his face into Montrose's like a dog about to bite. 'Do not think all sins go unpunished in this life, Montrose.'

Montrose attempted a smile, but his eyes flickered away to the contestants. 'Well, I see one set soon to be paid for.' As if reassured by the sight, he returned his gaze to Argyll. 'Will you not take my odds, Argyll? I give you five on the fop.'

Argyll glanced back to where Rob and Cunningham

had moved to the middle of the floor. He looked Montrose straight in the eye. 'I wager you but this. If McGregor lives, you will acquit him of all he owes you.'

For once in his life, Montrose was genuinely surprised. 'And if he loses?'

'I'll pay his bill.'

Something twisted in Montrose at this and he chose to recall an earlier occasion: 'My factor will call on your Lordship's factor.' He turned away and walked off as Argyll stared after him.

Cunningham and Rob were now face to face, with a referee standing between them. There was silence as the referee called out, 'Are we prepared?' The two protagonists barely nodded, and he continued, 'And agreed that all terms are set aside save victory?'

Rob said nothing, but Cunningham with a thin smile managed to croak, 'No quarter, asked or given.'

As the referee stepped aside there was more than a hint of concern on Argyll's face. Montrose stared at Cunningham with something resembling bafflement and curiosity. The two men raised their blades, the referee called, and they laid to.

At once the difference in style was obvious. Cunningham was dynamic and like quicksilver in his movements; his rapier quivering like a tongue, he was everywhere, moving from side to side with a taut, balletic balance. In contrast Rob seemed stolid, almost flat-footed, as he watched and waited with his heavy, two-handed weapon, presenting a very large and almost stationary target.

There was not a sound to be heard from among the watchers. Suddenly, Cunningham attacked with a flurry of movement, his blade probing, feinting, cutting. Rob managed to parry several of these strikes but soon one of them traced a swift red line on his forearm before he could manage to deflect it. Cunningham gave no respite and was in again at once, and it was only by dint of several defensive strokes that Rob kept him back. Now it was Rob who was on the attack, thrusting once, twice then making a swing. Cunningham quickly backed out of range, but not before he had struck Rob a blow across the shoulder drawing blood and a sharp hiss from the crowd.

It seemed clear now how things would go. Rob was crouching behind his sword, and he felt it too as he watched the elusive target with its deadly accuracy of attack. Cunningham seemed to have lost any qualms he might ever have had about the outcome. He settled down to enjoy the bout, switching his sword from hand to hand, feinting, holding back, walking a little strut to the side then coming in swiftly, thrusting three times, each one a little closer to the mark and finishing with a slash to Rob's neck which drew further blood.

Rob waited. Cunningham's eyes held him, willing him to acknowledge that it was just a matter of time. Argyll's face was grave, while Montrose looked away as the inevitability of the outcome became more and more obvious.

Cunningham came in again, two feints and then a

long; deadly thrust. Rob let him strike but as he did so, drew back almost out of range. The point of the rapier pierced his chest, but then, freeing his left hand from the basket of the broadsword, Rob seized Cunningham's blade and held on to it.

Cunningham was surprised rather than apprehensive and tried to jerk free. Even though the blade was now cutting his hand, Rob held on tenaciously, blood seething through his clenched fingers. Cunningham began to realize that he was effectively disarmed, and his eyes met Rob's as the broadsword swung heavily down on the juncture between neck and shoulder. He cried out, but the blow had severed his throat and he uttered mere gouts of blood. Only when Cunningham had finally fallen away did Rob release the blade from his gashed hand, which he closed tight on itself. He looked once at the jerking figure sprawled on the floor before he turned and walked away.

Montrose stared at Cunningham, disbelieving, as he half took in the voice of Argyll: 'I will hold you to our bargain.' He continued to stare for a moment, then silently backed away.

Argyll went over to Rob and examined his hand. 'That will need care.'

Rob nodded. 'I will go where it can be found, by Your Lordship's leave.' Rob's eyes were steady and without any hint of pleading.

Argyll looked at him and shrugged. 'As you please . . . I will know to wager on you the next time, McGregor.'

'Your Grace should live so long . . .' He turned and

made his exit with as little formality as he had his entrance.

Outside the house at Glen Shirra, Mary was carrying a basket of washing down to the burn. Slightly breathless, she settled down at the water's edge and began to sort out the clothing. Distracted for a moment, she was staring into the pool and watching the dark backs of the trout flicking from side to side, when high up on the hillside behind there came a shout. Startled, she looked up. It was the boys running on down the valley of the burn. She stared into the sunlight, shading her eyes.

The boys ran along the burn, jumping and tumbling, as Mary turned to see where they were heading. Far, far below, a tall figure was exhaustedly making its way slowly up the hillside. She knew who it was, and started off at a run herself.

In seconds she was almost up with the boys, as Rob came up the glen bearing his bloody fist before him like a trophy.

And, had it been thy lot to live
With us who now behold the light,
Thou wouldst have nobly stirred thyself,
And battled for the Right.

For thou wert still the poor man's stay,
The poor man's heart, the poor man's hand;
And all the oppressed who wanted strength,
Had thine at their command.

Bear witness many a pensive sigh
Of thoughtful Herdsman when he strays
Alone upon Loch Veol's heights,
And by Loch Lomond's braes.

And far and near, through vale and hill,
Are faces that attest the same;
The proud heart flashing through the eyes,
At sound of ROB ROY's name.

– *Rob Roy's Grave*
William Wordsworth

EPILOGUE

An historical postscript

A true account anent the person and character of the outlaw and brigand commonly known as 'Rob Roy'.

'Rob Roy' (1671–1734) was by descent a McGregor, being the younger son of Donald McGregor of Glengyle, a lieutenant-colonel in the army of James II (of Britain), by his wife, a daughter of William Campbell of Gleneaves. He was given the name 'Roy' (Gaelic = 'red') on account of his auburn hair, and latterly adopted the name of Campbell as his surname on account of the name McGregor being proscribed. Though in stature not much above middle height, he was so muscular and thickly set that few were his equals in feats of strength while the extraordinary length of his arms gave him a prodigious advantage in the use of the sword. His eyes were piercing, and with his whole expression formed an appropriate complement to his powerful physical frame. He, by way of inheritance, came into a small property on the Braes of Balquhidder and at first devoted himself to the rearing of cattle. Having formed a band of armed clansmen, he obtained, after the accession of William III (in 1689), a commission from the King in Exile, James II, to levy war on all who refused to acknowledge the latter as rightful monarch. In the autumn of 1691 he made a descent on the county of Stirlingshire to carry off the cattle of Lord Livingstone, when, being opposed by the villagers of Kippen, he also seized cattle from all the byres in the village. Shortly thereafter he married Helen Mary, daughter of McGregor of Comar. On the death of Gregor McGregor, the chief of the clan, in 1693, he managed, though not the nearest heir, to get himself acknowledged chief, obtaining control of the lands stretching from the Braes of Balquhidder to the shores of Loch Lomond and situated between the possessions of Argyll and Montrose. To assist in carrying on his trade as a cattle-dealer he borrowed money from the first Duke of Montrose, and being unable to repay it, he was evicted from his property and declared an outlaw. Taking refuge in the more inaccessible parts of the Highlands, Rob Roy from this time forward supported himself chiefly by depredations committed in the most daring manner on the said Duke and his tenants, all attempts to capture him being unsuccessful. During the uprising of 1715, though nominally siding with the Jacobite cause, he did not take an active part in the Battle of Sherrifmuir. His name was included in the Act of Attainder, but, having for some time enjoyed the friendship of the Duke of Argyll, he obtained, on making his submission at Inveraray, a promise of protection. Ultimately, through the mediation of Argyll, he was reconciled to Montrose, and in 1722 made submission to General Wade. He was carried off and imprisoned in Newgate and in 1727 was pardoned just as he was about to be transported to Barbados. He returned to Scotland and, according to a notice in the *Caledonian Mercury*, died at Balquhidder on 28 December 1734. He lies buried in Balquhidder kirk-yard.

More Compelling Fiction from Headline:

P.C. DOHERTY

AN ANCIENT EVIL

THE KNIGHT'S TALE OF MYSTERY AND MURDER AS HE GOES ON PILGRIMAGE FROM LONDON TO CANTERBURY

As the travellers gather in the Tabard Inn at the start of a pilgrimage to pray before the blessed bones of St Thomas à Becket in Canterbury, they agree eagerly to mine host Harry's suggestion of amusing themselves on each day of their journey with one tale and each evening with another – but the latter to be of mystery, terror and murder. The Knight begins that evening: his tale opens with the destruction of a sinister cult at its stronghold in the wilds of Oxfordshire by Sir Hugo Mortimer during the reign of William the Conqueror and then moves to Oxford some two hundred years later where strange crimes and terrible murders are being committed. The authorities seem powerless but Lady Constance, Abbess of the Convent of St Anne's, believes the murders are connected with the legends of the cult and she petitions the King for help.

As the murders continue unabated, special commissioner Sir Godfrey Evesden and royal clerk Alexander MacBain uncover clues that lead to a macabre world sect, which worships the dark lord. But they can find no solution to a series of increasingly baffling questions and matters are not helped by the growing rift between Sir Godfrey and McBain for the hand and favour of the fair Lady Emily.

P.C. Doherty's previous novels (medieval mysteries featuring Hugh Corbett) are also available from Headline: SATAN IN ST MARY'S, CROWN IN DARKNESS, SPY IN CHANCERY, THE ANGEL OF DEATH, THE PRINCE OF DARKNESS, MURDER WEARS A COWL, THE ASSASSIN IN THE GREENWOOD;

'Medieval London comes vividly to life...Doherty's depictions of medieval characters and manners of thought, from the highest to the lowest in the land, ringing true'
Publishers Weekly

FICTION/CRIME 0 7472 4356 5

More Crime Fiction from Headline:

THE WHITE ROSE MURDERS

BEING THE FIRST JOURNAL OF SIR ROGER SHALLOT CONCERNING CERTAIN WICKED CONSPIRACIES AND HORRIBLE MURDERS PERPETRATED IN THE REIGN OF KING HENRY VIII

MICHAEL CLYNES

In 1517 the English armies have defeated and killed James IV of Scotland at Flodden and James's widow-queen, Margaret, sister to Henry VIII, has fled to England, leaving her crown under a Council of Regency.

Shallot is drawn into a web of mystery and murder by his close friendship with Benjamin Daunbey, the nephew of Cardinal Wolsey, first minister of Henry VIII. Benjamin and Roger are ordered into Margaret's household to resolve certain mysteries as well as to bring about her restoration to Scotland.

They begin by questioning Selkirk, a half-mad physician imprisoned in the Tower. He is subsequently found poisoned in a locked chamber guarded by soldiers. The only clue is a poem of riddles. However, the poem contains the seeds for other gruesome murders. The faceless assassin always leaves a white rose, the mark of *Les Blancs Sangliers*, a secret society plotting the overthrow of the Tudor monarchy...

FICTION/CRIME 0 7472 3785 9